Golf Course Cutie

AND

Be Afraid

two Haven Port Island stories

Donna Lee Anderson

BLUE FORGE PRESS
Port Orchard, Washington

Be Afraid
Copyright 2019
by Donna Lee Anderson

Golf Course Cutie
Copyright 2019
by Donna Lee Anderson

First eBook Edition March 2021
First Print Edition March 2021

ISBN 978-1-59092-955-1

For information about film, reprint or other subsidiary rights, contact blueforgegroup@gmail.com

Blue Forge Press is the print division of the volunteer-run, federal 501(c)3 nonprofit company, Blue Forge Group, founded in 1989 and dedicated to bringing light to the shadows and voice to the silence. We strive to empower storytellers across all walks of life with our four divisions: Blue Forge Press, Blue Forge Films, Blue Forge Gaming, and Blue Forge Records. Find out more at www. BlueForgeGroup.org

Blue Forge Press
7419 Ebbert Drive Southeast
Port Orchard, Washington 98367
blueforgepress@gmail.com
360-550-2071 ph.txt

*in loving memory of
Donna Lee Anderson*

Golf Course Cutie

and

Be Afraid

two Haven Port Island stories

Donna Lee Anderson

GOLF COURSE COURSE

CUTIE

CHAPTER 1

Clyde was hoping to find someone he knew in the ferry line. On the Washington State ferries that leave Seattle, both drivers and passengers pay a fee, but if he could find someone that had already paid for a car, and that was already in line, well he might be able to talk them into a ride for free.

He'd almost given up when he ran into Sam. They'd gone to school together at Haven Port Island High, but Clyde hadn't seen Sam since those old baseball team days.

Sam was standing by his car smoking when Clyde walked up. "Hey Sam. Long time no see." Clyde was smiling and holding out his hand.

Sam turned and took the offered hand as he blew smoke out his nose and mouth. "Yea, has been. What you up to?"

Clyde lowered his voice. "Well, I'm a little down

on my luck and looking for a way to get back to Haven Port. Would you consider giving me a ride?"

Sam took a moment to take a last drag on the cigarette and throw it down. As he ground it out with his heel he said, "Sure, why not. Get in." He looked at his watch. "The ferry is about ready to load."

So that's how Clyde happened to be in the woods across from the high school, on Haven Port Island, on a Wednesday afternoon.

During his usual rounds of the island, Sheriff Ken Owens usually drove down this road to check these woods. Some of the high school kids had built a fire there a few weeks ago and after it was put out, Sheriff Owens did a little peripheral checking and noticed there was a dug out space in an area about a hundred and fifty feet into these trees. It was a small hill and on the far side, away from the street, someone had scooped out enough dirt so a person or two could go into this cave and sit, or lay. Some old plywood was on the floor with cardboard up the sides of the walls. All in all, it was only about eight feet deep and around three feet high but the Sheriff checked it every few days. Today he was surprised to find a backpack in there and a sleeping man.

"Hey. You can't sleep here," said the Sheriff as he tapped the bottom of the man's shoes.

There was a snuffling sound and then Clyde sat up. "Why not. I'm not hurting nothin'."

"That's not the point. The point is that this is not a camp ground and you are camping."

"No I'm not. No. Not camping. Just taking a nap. Do I have to leave now?"

"Yes you do. What is your name?"

"Clyde. Clyde Cousteau." And this is when the Sheriff recognized him. "My folks used to have a place on the Cliffs and I went to school here. Folks are gone now and so is the buddy I was supposed to stay with. Sorry if I broke a law. I just wanted to get some sleep before I started out again."

"Where will you go?

"Probably back to Seattle."

The Sheriff had heard these kinds of stories before, but not directly from Clyde. "Where specifically?"

"There's a residence for guys like me down by the waterfront so I'll go there until I can make a better plan."

"Sounds like an idea. Can you get down to the ferry okay?"

"Yep. Now that I'm awake, I'll get going." Clyde started to stand up then realized he couldn't because of the low roof, so he grabbed his backpack and crawled out of the cave. "Don't suppose you could give me a ride down to the ferry, could you?"

Clyde was not a little man. At five-foot-eleven he wasn't considered short, but when he straightened up next to the Sherriff's six-foot-three he didn't feel all that big.

"Well Clyde, you are in luck. That just happens to be where I'm heading, but you'll have to ride in the back seat."

"Suits me. And thanks for the favor."

Both men came out of the woods and as Sheriff Owens got in the driver's side, Clyde got in the back seat, happy not to have to walk the even the few blocks back to the ferry dock.

On the way back from delivering his passenger, Ken Owens stopped at Murph's Place, a local restaurant and bar by the golf course.

"Hi Murph," he said as he came in. "Got any coffee?"

"Hello Ken. Sure do. Have a seat."

Murph and Ken had been friends since they went to high school together, here on the island. Murph poured the coffee and said, "What brings you into our place?"

"You won't believe who is or was back here on the island. Clyde Cousteau. Found him in the woods by the high school. Someone has a cave built in the side of a small hill about in the middle of the woods and there he was. Snoozin'."

"Oh crap. Not Clyde. When's he leaving?"

"I just dropped him off at the ferry dock and a ferry was coming in. He's supposed to be on it back to Seattle."

"Good riddance. Did he say why he was here?"

"This is what I gathered: Clyde's folks used to live here. This I knew of course. Today he came over to stay with a friend but for some reason he can't. He didn't tell me the reason but he sure smells bad and he looks homeless to me."

"Glad he left. He's nothing but trouble. Remember him and his brother?" said Murph.

Ken said, "Of course I do. All the drinking and drugs and stealing they did, and the way they treated the girls. Then there was the Raccoon races. How could I forget?"

Ken and Murph and the Cousteau boys were all students at Haven Port High at the same time. Ken and Murph were seniors and the Cousteau boys were both freshmen. They were born a year apart but one got set back in grade school so they ended up in the same grade for most of their schooling. The Raccoon races were their idea of fun. They would catch raccoons, cut off their back feet and then have races to see which one could get the farthest before it collapsed.

"When he was here before and causing all those problems with the raccoons and other stuff, I found out neither of them graduated. I think the school just got so tired of all the problems they caused that they gave them both GED's and opted them out of the school system."

Murph was rubbing the perpetual sore spot on his back where he still carried the bullet they couldn't remove and said, "I heard the bother died and I'm glad Clyde left here. Hope he never comes back to stay."

Ken took a last drink of coffee, laid a dollar on the bar and stood up as he said, "Me too. See ya' soon, Murph."

Murph watched as Ken left and through the glass door, he could see him getting into his squad car. Boy he really, really agreed with the Sheriff and wished Clyde was gone for sure. Not only was he mean when he drank, he was also cruel as he proved when he mutilated animals for fun. Murph thought again, *Good riddance.*

CHAPTER 2

S ee you tomorrow Bibb," said Murph. He was a happy man. An old partner of his from the Seattle Police Department was just leaving and they had agreed on a plan.

James Bibber, Bibb to his Seattle Police Department and military and school friends, was also a happy man. Murph and Bibb had just settled on a deal. Bibb was coming to work at Murph's Place. He'd been working in Seattle in a restaurant tending bar but wanted to move back to Haven Port, so here he was applying for a job that Murph was so happy to give him. Now there would be days off for Murph and he was ready for that to happen.

Bibb would start tomorrow. They'd work together for a few days so Bibb could see how Murph wanted things done, and then Murph would be able to take his lady friend Lisa out for lunch and maybe even dinner, or have a week-end together.

The regular crew was sitting at the bar. Steve and George and Larry from St. Joseph's Retirement Home, along with Murph's old boss Joe Westover from the Westover Real Estate office in Seattle.

"Hey Murph, hear any more about that woman they found dead on the golf course?" Joe took a drink from his beer. "I haven't heard any details since they accused that neighbor."

"I haven't heard anything new either," said Murph. "They let that neighbor woman go. No evidence and although there was no love lost, she didn't kill the girl and throw her body in that sand trap. First of all, she's not big enough or strong enough to do the throwing, and although she was mad at the girl, she doesn't seem the type to murder her."

Joe laughed. "I lived in the next block and I've known that woman and her family for years. I agree she probably wouldn't kill her but she does have a temper. One time she chased a salesman brandishing a meat cleaver. He was trying to sell her a vacuum cleaner then made a move on her. Story goes that she picked up the meat cleaver from the kitchen counter and not only chased him out of the house and yard but half way up the block."

Larry poked Steve in the side. "Ever been chased with a meat cleaver?"

Steve was smiling. "Nope. Never got anyone

that mad. I'm a lot smoother than that."

All four of the men were laughing and so was Murph when he said to Steve, "Ever get chased by anyone because of your amorous moves?"

"Now you know I don't tell stories about my love adventures, but..." Steve started to laugh and so did everyone within hearing. Steven Edward Xavier was well known for the sharing of his romantic adventures and perhaps embellishing the circumstances so much that hardly anyone believed his stories. However, truth be told, most of the stories were very true. "There was the time when a bull dog decided I wasn't welcome any more and caused me to quickly vacate the premises. He took exception to his mistress' screams and took them to be of the un-happy sort when indeed they were of the VERY HAPPY sort." Now everyone was laughing again, and Steve was smiling broadly.

Murph moved away from these guys and re-filled the coffee cups for the couple at the table by the window, and then took food orders from the group of three ladies and a teen-aged boy that had just come in. When he returned from the kitchen, Joe motioned him to come over.

"Got a request for you," said Joe. "We got a listing of one of the houses up by the fire station, and I need someone to give it an inspection." He adjusted his tie. "Want someone to see what, if any, repairs it needs before it's ready to sell. It's a pretty old structure. Would you have time to check it out?"

"Why do you need me? You're here so why not do it yourself?"

"Well, that's just the thing. I was supposed to meet someone there to see the place today but no one showed up. I have their name and number and I called them but they had the days mixed up and won't be here until tomorrow. The problem is I can't come back tomorrow so I was wondering if you would be able to do it. Four o'clock tomorrow and here's the address. I'll pay you your old rate for appraisals." Joe was looking at Murph with almost a pleading look in his eyes.

"Well, I guess I could go take a look," said Murph. Now that Bibb was going to be here, he could take some time away from his bar now and then, and that made him smile. He took the paper Joe was handing him and they shook hands.

Joe got off the bar stool and stood up. "Thanks Murph. Just give me a call with a verbal and then we can do the paperwork." He started for the door and was hitching up his pants, like he always did when his plans went well.

Murph looked at the address. It was on the corner of Apple Avenue and Hardy. He thought he knew the house he would be seeing, and was looking forward to spending some time doing this job. It wasn't that he didn't like the bar business, but seven days a week, sixteen hours a day was starting to wear thin. Murph felt a little guilty being so happy to get away from here, but then he reminded himself, *all work and no play, makes Murph a boring boy.*

CHAPTER 3

The next day Murph was a happy man again. Bibb was a natural as a bartender, just as Murph had hoped. He talked to the patrons, laughed with the cooks, and generally settled in to be part of the gang after the first hour. At three-thirty Murph left the bar and drove down Willow Street to Monroe Avenue and turned left. When he got to Apple Avenue he turned right and there on the corner of Apple and Hardy was the house he remembered. Back in the days when he was in high school and on the football team, he'd spent many warm evenings sitting on the porch with Rita. He briefly wondered where Rita was now-a-days and made a mental note to find out.

As Murph was parking in front of the house, a pickup truck came up behind him. The old green Chevy parked. A man wearing a baseball cap, and a long straggly, dirty gray beard got out of it. His jeans had not seen the laundry room for a long time. His shirt was unbuttoned showing a khaki colored undershirt and it was flapping against his legs as he walked. "I'm Slim," said the man. "I'm looking to sell this place."

"Hello. I'm Michael Murphy and I'm representing the real estate office. Came to do an appraisal." As they shook hands, Murph almost took a step back because of the strong breath coming from this man. Then when Slim smiled he could see only three broken and rotting teeth. Two on the bottom and one on top.

"Do you live here on the island now?" asked Murph.

Slim smiled his almost toothless smile and said, "Heck no. I live in Tacoma. This was my Mother's place and now that she's dead, I want to get rid of it." He reached in his pants pocket and pulled out a single key. "Let's get this done so I can get the next ferry home."

They went up the walk and when Slim opened the door, they could hear snoring coming from inside.

CHAPTER 4

The sound was coming from the living room area. The two men quickly followed it and there on the floor with throw pillows under his head and an afghan over him was a man, fast asleep and snoring very loudly.

Slim walked over and kicked the sleeping man's legs.

After a snort, the man quickly sat up. He looked at the guy standing over him and said, "Why'd you kick me?"

Slim said, "Why're you asleep in my house?"

Murph said, "Let's call the sheriff and have him handle this."

Slim said, "Yea. Do that. I don't want to spend my energy whopping up on him."

As he reached in his jacket pocket for his phone the man on the floor stood up and said, "Don't do that.

I was just sleeping in a dry place. I'll leave."

"How'd you get in?" asked Slim.

"Through the cellar door. It wasn't locked and I didn't take nothin'. All I did was sleep."

"How long you been here?" asked Murph. His policeman's training kicking in.

"What time is it?"

Murph looked at his watch. "A little after four in the afternoon."

"Been here since around noon. Sorry if I scared you guys but I'll leave now and ..."

Slim said, "Okay. Get your sorry ass out of here and never come back. If you do, I'll have my shot gun with me and you might be sorry."

The man picked up his back-pack and put his hat on his head as he headed for the front door. "Thank you guys." And he didn't slam the door when he left. Just closed it and casually walked down the steps of the porch and headed toward the corner.

"Wasn't no one checking on my Mom's place?" asked Slim.

"I don't really know but I'll check, and I'll make sure the cellar door is locked too.

Slim nodded in agreement then said, "Where do we start for this appraising stuff?"

"Might as well start here," and Murph took out his pen and the notebook he had in his pocket and the appraisal began.

Slim wanted to sell the house as-is. No repairs or fixes and if the buyer wanted the furniture that could be part of the deal. He also said he was going to take some of the personal stuff with him today, or as much as he could get into his truck. "She had lots of clothes and I took most of them the last time I was here. And I took some of the food but there is still the stuff in the pantry, and in her bathroom, and in the closet where she stored the towels and sheets for the beds. Stuff like that. I brought big plastic storage bags to put things in and when we're finished I'll go get 'em."

Murph didn't smile but he wanted to. "If you want to do that while I walk around and look at the other rooms, it would work for me."

Slim gave Murph a slow look—up and down—then said, "Okay. I guess I can trust you. I'll go get the bags," and he headed for the door.

The next hour was spent with Slim making frequent trips back and forth from the house to the truck. Evidently he'd forgotten to look in the chest-of-drawers when he took the clothing so that took a couple of trips along with all the canned good from the pantry. It seems that Slim's Mom was somewhat of a food hoarder and there were cases of canned milk, eight in total, and canned corn and string beans, five each, and then several more cases of things like ready-made frosting in a can, and cake mixes.

Murph was finished looking in the house and basement, which was really a cellar with concrete walls but a dirt floor, before he realized the sleeping guy was Clyde. He'd have to remember to tell Ken about this.

He found Slim in the kitchen pantry loading up a wheel barrow with several cases of canned fruit. "I'm finished inside so I think I take a look around the outside of the building."

Slim only glanced up and said, "Okay. My pickup is pretty full so I think I'll come back another time and get the rest of this stuff."

"What more are you taking, besides the food?"

"Well, my wife want's the bed clothes and the towels and the rugs, and when I come back I'll bring her so she can make sure she gets anything else she wants. Probably come back tomorrow if it's alright with you."

"The house is still yours until you sign the papers with the real estate firm. Maybe you could contact them and make arrangements to do that so they can sell this house and get you the money." Murph had the feeling that was what this guy really wanted.

"Okay. I'll do that and I'm gonna leave now. Back tomorrow but I'll call them real estate people and get that part started," and he headed out the kitchen door with his full wheel barrow and bumped down the one step into the yard.

Murph locked the door behind Slim. He'd already locked the cellar door and then he went out the front door, making sure it locked behind him. If someone wanted to sleep here again they would have to work at getting back in.

CHAPTER 5

lyde was walking along thinking about food. *Ham and eggs would be good.* He should have eaten some of the stuff in the refrigerator before he went to sleep in that house. He'd make sure he checked that out before sleeping next time.

When he left the house he walked down to the corner and then turned and went by the high school. No good memories there but he had seen a house for sale sort of tucked in behind the car-repair garage in the middle of the next block. He wanted to check out the possibility of a place to crash for tonight so that's where he headed.

The garage mechanic was loading up his tools into his van and as Clyde watched he drove off. It was almost five so Clyde supposed it was the end of the work day for the mechanic and he crossed the street to start his reconnaissance of the little house with the For Sale sign on it.

CHAPTER 6

On his way back to his bar, Murph thought about how much he liked to do appraisal work. While he was with the Seattle Police Department, but before he'd gotten shot and had to resign, his lady friend Lisa was trying to talk him into coming to work where she worked full time. Her boss was looking for an in-house appraiser of houses and property and she was worried his job would get him hurt. Well his job did result in a gun-shot to his back and that forced his retirement. During his hospital stay and recuperation, Lisa brought him books that would teach him real estate rules and the criteria for appraising. After he was mostly mobile again, he did go to work for Joe at the Westover Real Estate Office in Seattle. He did some selling but mostly appraisal work. Then the bar came up for sale and Murph's life changed again. Now he lived here on the island, above the restaurant/bar, and Lisa visited and stayed sometimes, but that too could change since he'd now be able to leave sometimes.

As he pulled into the parking lot of Murph's Place he decided he wasn't ready to give this up. Not yet. Someday maybe, but certainly not yet. He was still enjoying the people that were customers and the discussions that happened in the bar too much. And that reminded him about the girl that had been found on the golf course and he hoped the sheriff would come by soon and fill him in with details.

CHAPTER 7

The girl's body on the golf course had been found by early morning maintenance crew. Now it was at the doctor's office that handled any of Haven Port Island's bodies found under suspicious circumstances. There weren't very many of these cases but at the medical center there happened to be a semi-retired doctor that had been a Medical Examiner in California and when he retired he came back to Haven Port, where he'd grown up. He handled all the bodies that needed this special attention.

Sheriff Ken walked in the door at the clinic side of the medical building and took the elevator up to Dr. John Curran's office. Dr. Curran was pretty bald now but when he went to high school here on the island with Ken, he had curly, wild, un-kempt hair he chose not to cut nor did he comb it very often. All his buddies and most of the girls in the school called him Curly, and that's what he was still called now, by almost everyone.

The receptionist picked up the phone and checked with the doctor, then directed the Sheriff to go into the Doctor's office.

"Hi Curly. Got any news for me?" asked Ken as he entered the office.

Curly was sitting at his desk and reached behind him to pull a piece of paper out of the printer. "Not much but some. She was probably killed around 1:00AM. She was choked and then her neck was broken. She was naked except for socks, and only her bra was found under her. She was about thirty-five years old, blond by request, five foot six inches, and weighed one-hundred-nine. Need more?"

"Yea. It's been rumored she lived next door to Selma Rouge and they didn't get along but we sent Selma home. She's now seventy years old and I doubt she'd have the strength to do the damage that happened." Ken shifted in his chair as he reached for the paper Curly was handing him.

"I also found out she was sexually active that night. We found two different semen in the testing we did. Either a busy girl or two guys were there," said Curly as he took off his glasses. "And, one more bizarre thing, one of her nipples were cut off." He moved his chair closer to the desk and then said, "Got any leads?"

"Wish we did," said Ken. He was trying to

digest this new news about the mutilation too. "Don't even know when she got back to the island. She's been gone a couple of years, at least that's what her old neighbor Selma told us. Her parents both moved about a year ago and Selma doesn't know where any of them live now. They were renters so don't even have that avenue to go down."

"Well someone knows. Just hope they're still on the island, or maybe I hope they aren't." Curly smiled. "Be better if someone would just email us a confession, wouldn't it?"

Ken stood up. "Yep. Sure would. See you later, Curly," and he walked out the door and took the stairs down and back to his squad car.

CHAPTER 8

Clyde was here on the island to see Eddy, one of his old gambling buddies. He thought maybe he could get back the money he'd lent Eddy, but the place Clyde knew to be his house had been torn down and an apartment building stood in its place. The manager didn't know this Eddy guy, so that was the end of that. No Eddy, no money and *maybe no place to sleep tonight*. Clyde smiled as he thought this. There was always a place to sleep. He just had to find it.

The house behind the mechanic's shop turned out to be a possibility. It could to be a sleeping place. Clyde found an unlocked window by the back door and once inside he even found a bed. Looked like tonight he'd be sleeping like people should. On a bed and for a stretch of at least eight hours.

Clyde set his back-pack by the back door, handy

just in case, and decided he'd go look for some food before he crashed. This refrigerator was empty and had been turned off so he would have to look somewhere else for eats, and he hadn't really slept for any length of time since last Sunday, but tonight would be his catching-up time. Then tomorrow he'd try to find Eddy, and if that didn't work out, then he'd go back to Seattle to the shelter. This was about the farthest Clyde's plan ever went. Maybe twenty-four hours ahead, but not much more. 'No sense making plans that always changed' was his opinion.

CHAPTER 9

At the Airport Café that was on the east side of Haven Port, the crowd was starting to gather. It was a working man's bar and also sold food. Not fancy food but things like hamburgers and hot dogs and breakfasts. You could get a breakfast any time from six in the morning until they closed at ten that night. Clyde had been there many times and was hoping some of his old buddies would be there too, so that's where he was headed.

As he got close to the parking lot, he looked at the vehicles to see if he recognized any. He was especially looking for Eddy's truck but didn't see it. *Maybe he just isn't here yet*, he thought.

The door was propped open and Clyde walked into a noisy, smoky room atmosphere and could hear the pool table sounds from the back. It made him smile. Good sounds to him. They made him feel he was home.

The bar was on the right side from the door and he walked over and sat on a stool. When the bartender came over Clyde ordered a beer.

"What kind do ya' want?" came the question.

"Whatever is the cheapest," was his reply, and the bartender stooped down and opened a small cooler to his left. "Here you go buddy. One dollar," he said as he flipped the cap off bottle and onto the floor.

Clyde put his hand in his pocket and come up with a hand full of change. He put it on the bar and started counting. "Twenty-five, fifty, sixty, sixty-five, seventy-five, one dollar." He pushed the change he'd separated over to the bar keep and scooped the rest of it up and put it back in his pocket.

As he picked up the beer and took a drink he thought, *Not too bad*.

As he took another drink he turned to survey the room and who might be here that he'd know. All of his family had moved away but you never knew who might be left from his school and growing up days. As he looked around Daryl came in with another guy. They both went directly toward the Men's Room and when Daryl came out he too looked around to see if any of his crowd was here yet. That's when his eyes looked at Clyde and he started towards him.

"How you doin' fella'? Daryl said as he approached.

"Just doin' what I can," said Clyde. "Hopin' I'd see you around."

"Yeah? I just got off work. Got a job in construction. Building a barn right now. Where you been?"

Clyde looked down at the floor. It was time for him to ask for help and that meant he needed to look humble. "Just got fired from a waterfront guard job. Seems there was a boat that got stolen and I didn't know it was happening." He looked up at Daryl to see his reaction.

"Did you make any money on the boat deal?"

"No. The guy that stole it was a son of the owner so it was a very quiet job. I didn't even know it was missing until the owner came to use it and it was gone. They didn't think I was involved but they said they needed someone with more boat experience so it didn't happen again and I was fired."

"Bummer," said Daryl. "What you gonna do now?"

"Don't know. Find a place to crash for a few days while I look around. Got any ideas for me?"

Daryl took off his stained and dirty baseball cap and wiped his wrist across his forehead. "Might be you could apply where I'm working. Want to go in tomorrow with me?"

Clyde smiled. "That would be great. Where should we meet?"

"If you want to you can stay at my place tonight."

That's what Clyde was waiting for and visibly relaxed. "That would be great. How long you gonna be here?"

"Couple of hours, but if you need to stop and get something we could do that on the way home. We thought we'd have something to eat then play a little pool. Want to hang out with us and then I'll take you home with me?"

Daryl was smiling and so was Clyde. This was happening just like Clyde hoped it would.

CHAPTER 10

At six o'clock that evening at the sheriff's office, Ken was getting ready to go home. The office was essentially closed after this hour but in case any of the deputies wanted or needed to contact him, Ken always had his phone turned on and with him. Ethan Mitchell and Andy Andrews were the deputies, and Charlie Carlisle the office manager. They were not really standing at attention but they were standing in front of him, paying attention as Sheriff Ken Owens told them about finding Clyde in the cave. He also told them to pay attention if there were any break-ins or thefts around town the next couple of days. "I dropped this guy at the ferry and he was supposed to leave for Seattle, but I couldn't wait until the ferry left and I'm not sure I can trust that he's gone."

The three guys all nodded in understanding and then, since it was time to close the office, they all said their 'good-nights' and left for the night. Andy went home to his wife and two children, Charlie went home to his girl-friend, and Ethan went home to his apartment.

"See you all tomorrow," said the Sheriff as they left, and since he was the last man out, he paused and locked the office door. Never thinking what a busy day tomorrow was about to come.

CHAPTER 11

Murph opened the bar and restaurant as usual at six on this Friday morning. Many golf players were used to stopping for breakfast before they continued on down the block to the golf course. Of course the news about the girl that was found dead in a sand trap was a big topic of conversation.

"Heard the girl was raped and strangled and was very bloody. Know anything about that Murph?"

Murph was pouring coffee at a table of four men who'd come in on the five-fifty-five ferry this morning. They were headed for the golf course and the week-end tournament that started today.

Another guy chimed in and said, "Hope they got that trap all cleaned out or Bill here might get stuff all over his balls."

Bill smiled and said, "I don't get in any more traps than you do but if I do, you can keep me company." All four of the men were laughing now and Murph just smiled to show he understood.

More golfers were coming into the restaurant and the new guy, Bibb that he had just been hired, was behind the bar, but he was also taking orders for food. At seven-thirty the room started to empty. Tee off time at the golf course started at eight and most of these golfers hadn't even signed in yet so their departure was not quiet, but it was fast.

By eight-thirty the tables were cleared and clean and both Bibb and Murph were ready for a sit-down and a cup of coffee. That's when Sheriff Ken came in. "Hello. Didn't expect to see you sitting with the golf tournament about to start."

"Yea. Wonder where the golfers are? Any idea Bibb?"

Bibb couldn't help laughing. He looked at Murph and said, "Too bad the sheriff couldn't have come in fifteen minutes earlier."

Murph said, "Yeah, Ken. You just missed the crowd."

Ken was smiling. "I thought so. Missing the crowd was what I was aiming at."

After they all stopped laughing, Murph said "Want some coffee?"

Ken nodded and Bibb filled a cup and set it in front of him.

Murph said, "Anything new on the girl at the

golf course?"

"Well, yes but I shouldn't talk about it."

"Oh come on. Tell us as one-cop-to-another." Both Bibb and Murph were looking at Ken.

"Okay. But I have to warn you, no one else is to know, okay?"

Both guys nodded and Ken said, "After we moved the girl's body we found an ID necklace. The kind the guys used to wear with dog-tag like pieces hanging from the chain. We're looking for the names of the men that were on them. Looks like military issue, and we found two different names on the tags, and they looked old. That's the latest."

Murph said, "Were there names on them did you say?"

"Yes, but the names weren't any we recognized from here. No locals. The FBI has them now and we should hear something in a couple of days. At least I'm hoping so."

Bibb said, "Remember that case in Seattle we worked on where the street walker collected guy's jewelry. She liked their necklaces best and she had probably twenty dog-tags of customers."

Murph smiled. "Yep I remember, and that the one that she liked the best was from a guy that was in Viet Nam and he was eighty some years old."

CHAPTER 12

At the golf course there was much conversation going on about the body being found too. The sand trap that was so interesting was at the end of Hole number 1, which was at the corner of the course and behind where the golfers teed off for Hole number 2. It had a tarp over it now.

Since this was only a nine-hole course, all the tournaments just played two rounds. When a player finished playing Hole number 9, they usually went into the club house either to make use of the necessary room, or to have a refreshment before starting the second half of the game.

Police tape was posted around the sand trap so everyone knew the story by the time they finished the first nine, and in the bar area, speculation was rampant.

As several of them were getting ready to go out

to play, two guys were still at a table talking. "I heard the gal was just laying there naked when the greens-keeper made his rounds this morning. She did have on one shoe and socks, but there weren't any other clothes or the other shoe by the body."

Another fellow said, "Do they know what killed her?"

"I guess they decided strangulation and stabbing. There was lots of blood but a piece of rope was still around her neck with knots tied in it so it hit her windpipe. Someone seems to have known what they were doing." They got up to go and finish their game and as they went out the door one of the guys said, "For a little place like Haven Port, they sure do have interesting stuff happening here."

CHAPTER 13

Clyde spent the night with his friend Daryl, and went to work with him the next morning at eight. The boss hired him as a laborer and put a shovel in his hand. "I need this pile of dirt loaded into that pickup bed and when it's all in there, I'll tell you where it needs to end up."

Being a shovel jockey wasn't Clyde's idea of a good time but what the heck, he didn't have any other plans, at least not until he could find the guy he really wanted to see.

By ten o'clock, the dirt pile and roots were all in the pickup. "Hey Clyde. Can you drive a pickup with a stick shift?" The boss had been paying attention to Clyde's shoveling and came out of his trailer.

"Yep. Learned to drive on a pickup sort of like this."

"Good. The keys are in it and I'll send Joe with

you to show you where they need fill dirt." The boss then turned away from Clyde and yelled, "Joe! Come over here!"

Joe was a little guy. He stood about five feet three and was really muscular. "Yeah?" he said as he approached.

"Clyde can drive this pickup and you know where the fill dirt is supposed to go so you go with him and help unload it. Okay?"

Joe looked at Clyde and decided it would be okay so he just said, "Yeah," and went to get into the truck. Joe watched him and said, "...take this shovel for him and then come back here. Be sure you finish this job before five o'clock. I don't want to get home late tonight."

Clyde threw both of the shovels into the back of the truck, and went to the driver's side. What a weird day this was turning out to be, but at least he'd get paid and he could really use come cash.

CHAPTER 14

Daryl was sitting in his truck when Clyde and Joe came back to the worksite. Joe got out of the pickup without saying a word and went to his own vehicle. Clyde got out too and locked the door and put the truck key in his pocket since the boss wasn't there. He walked over to where Daryl was waiting and said, "Now what?"

"The boss said he had work for you tomorrow too so he'll pay you then. Want to crash with me again?"

"I guess so but I don't have any money for eating or anything."

"I'll make sure you eat and you can sleep in the same place as last night. Let's go. I'm thirsty!" Clyde got into Daryl's truck and they were off to the same bar as last night. Beer was waiting.

They pulled into the parking lot and Daryl said, "Just run a tab and I'll pick it up when we go home." Clyde liked that idea and as they walked into the bar, the first thing he did was order a straight shot of whisky with a water back. After that he drank beer but that first drink got his motor running and he was the life of the party on the dance floor. Around ten o'clock Daryl sat down beside him at the bar and said, "Time to go home. Did you eat?"

"Nope. Was having too much fun!"

"Well, order a hamburger to go and let's go get some sleep. Six o'clock comes early on a work day."

Clyde ordered the hamburger with fries and as soon as it was delivered Daryl paid the bar bill and they left.

The next day was almost a carbon copy of the day before. Shovel dirt into the pickup, deliver the dirt and empty the pickup. Only difference was that Joe wasn't along. Clyde thought *this isn't the best job and not the worst, but wonder when I get paid?* At four thirty he was back at the job site and went to find the Boss. "Hey, when is payday around here?"

"Friday's. Why?"

"I'm sort of running on empty. Any chance I could get a loan against Friday?"

The Boss smiled. He'd hired these kind of guys off and on ever since he began doing this job so he understood. "I figure we owe you about $50. Would $25 help you make it through?"

Clyde said, "Well, $50 would make it a lot easier to last until pay day."

The Boss just looked at him, reached in his pocket and pulled out two twenty-dollar bills. "This is all I have here on the job. Can you make do?"

Clyde reached over and took the forty dollars. "Sure can. Thanks." And he walked over to the parking lot looking for Daryl.

That night Clyde was sitting at a table in the bar with a young woman and she was busy telling him about a girl that got killed at the golf course. He was very interested and ask as many questions as he thought he could without arousing suspicion. "Do they know who did it?"

"Not yet, but they think it was someone local."

"Why is that?"

"Because Becky was from here, and she's been known to have some dates out by that sand trap on the golf course. She doesn't really live here anymore but she comes over really a lot for dates."

"Where's she live? Is she ... was she a hooker?"

"No! She just liked to entertain out there and usually the guy she was with would pay her for the entertainment. I think she has a place in Seattle now."

Clyde nodded. *A hooker,* he thought, and

getting paid for entertaining wasn't a bad gig. Maybe he could use that sometime. "Do the police have any leads?"

"Don't know, but let's dance. I'm ready again, are you?"

And Clyde was ready.

CHAPTER 15

The sheriff's office was busy today. Sheriff Ken was on the phone with his former work-mate at the FBI office in Seattle for almost an hour, when the fax machine started spitting out papers. Deputy Mitchell was ready with a folder in hand, and was gathering the papers and putting them in order as fast as he could. Lucky for him the pages were numbered because a few times a page shot out of the machine and onto the floor.

Ken was watching this happen and decided that a new fax with a paper catcher was going to make its way into this office. No doubt Charlie, the office manager, would know how to work with it and he'd see to it that Ethan and Andy got taught how to use it too.

This FBI report that just came in didn't show anything too surprising. The dead girl was known in

Seattle as Becky Coop, one of the so called 'street-walkers' down by the waterfront and also around the Pike Street Market. She didn't have a permanent address but the FBI agent Ken talked to said she probably lived, or at least slept, at an old house at the base of Queen Anne hill, just north of the city. An old lady who was once quite well known in the prostitution crowd around Seattle about forty-years ago, had set up in this house to help those ladies-of-the-streets have a place to call their home. This place was really a mansion from the early nineteen-twenties and had been a boarding house, so that's why it had so many bedrooms. The report estimated there were twenty-seven of these bedrooms that were rented out like apartments, but there was no cooking in the rooms, nor was there a central dining room for the 'guests'. Someone had installed shower rooms but this house was really just a place for the women to crash after a hard days or nights work.

Ken put her name in his notebook and after he finished reading the report, he stood up, put on his jacket and picked up his hat. Now he had people to talk to about Miss Becky and why she was on Haven Port Island, and who she still knew here, or at least who her contacts were. As he came out of his office all three men on his staff looked up and two of them stood up at attention. Why this happened in the office Ken didn't know, and although he'd talked to them both, they still thought it was necessary to be standing at attention if the sheriff was in the room.

"Did any of you go to high school here?" All three men were in their late thirties and Ethan and Andy had gone to school here. "Did you know a Becky Coop?"

"Sure. She was a year behind of me and moved to Seattle in the middle of her Junior year," said Andy.

"I didn't know her," said Ethan.

"Andy could you tell me where she lived and the name of her parents?"

"Well, she was in a different crowd than I was. Her crowd did a lot of partying and drinking and going to Seattle on the weekends. I was into sports so my weekends were full of games. Don't remember them, her crowd, coming to any of the games. And I don't remember where she lived except it was under the cliffs."

Ken mentally shook his head. When he grew up on Haven Port Island and went to school here he could have told you where all the kids he knew lived, and especially the girls. He'd been into sports too but never too busy to know other kids, *but that was just me* he thought. *I wanted to know everything about everyone. That's probably why I ended up being recruited by the FBI.*

First stop for Ken was at Murph's Place. He'd decided to have lunch and see if Murph had heard anything more that might help. Gossip seemed to have a central place here.

Murph and Ken had gone to high school here on the island together and then to the University of Washington together. Murph ended up with the Seattle Police Department and Ken with the FBI in Philadephia, and both retired back here. Ken was thinking about this as he parked his car. This island was just crawling with retired FBI, policemen, and military officers and doctors. *No wonder because it's a nice place to live, but funny it attracted so many of us.*

Ken took a stool at the end of the bar and Bibb was on duty. "Hi Sheriff, coffee or a menu?"

"Think I'll just have a BLT and fries today. And coffee please," said Ken.

"Okie dokie," said Bibb as he picked up a cup and the coffee pot and moved down to where Ken was sitting. "Coming right up."

"Murph off having fun?" asked Ken.

"Don't know where he is but he'll be back any time now," said Bibb, the newest addition to Murph's staff was good at remembering faces and even the regulars felt like they knew him. "Said he had some business to do but wouldn't be gone long."

Also at the bar today were the semi-regular customers. St. Joseph's Retirement home was just a few block away and some of the residents made it a daily habit to take their walk down to Murph's, stop and have coffee or maybe a drink, then walk back home. Steve and George and Larry seemed to be fixtures at one o'clock every afternoon and here they were today.

Ken took a sip of coffee and then realized all three of the men sitting at the bar were looking at him. Steve waited for Ken to put down his cup then asked, "What's up with the Golf Course body?"

Ken said, "I don't know much yet. You guys hear anything?"

George shook his head no. Larry started to talk but Steve interrupted him. "We been waiting to hear something from you." Then Larry nodded no too, just as George was doing.

"This is what I know. The girl used to go to school here, then moved to Seattle. Did any of you know the Coop family?"

All three of them shook their head no. Then Steve said, "None of us lived here before we moved into the retirement home, but I bet Dr. Pete would know if anyone would."

Ken smiled. That was to his next stop after lunch. Dr. Pete was a retired GP from Seattle and now was the resident doctor at the retirement home, but he and his family had spent every summer here before that and he seemed to know everyone.

"Thanks. I'll check with him," said Ken.

As Bibb put his lunch plate down in front of him he said, "As I hear it, if Dr. Pete didn't know someone, they probably didn't exist." All the men laughed at his joke and Ken thought, *boy, ain't that the truth.*

Doctor Pete wasn't at St. Joseph's when Ken stopped there but Sister Nora said he'd be back at three o'clock so Ken decided to make a swing around to his own home to check on things. His wife hadn't been feeling to so good when he left this morning and maybe he could do something for her. He pulled into his driveway and noticed the front door was open. Not ajar, but full open. He hurried into the house and found his wife in the front room, television set blaring and fully asleep in her lounger chair. By her side was on the table was an empty glass, half a bottle of vodka and the remote was in her hand, in her lap.

He picked up the remote and turned off the TV then went and closed the door. None of this activity interfered with his wife's nap. He picked up the vodka bottle and took it back to the den and although he couldn't see the bottle top, he put it back in the liquor cupboard and looked for the lock that usually held the doors closed and secure. He found it on the floor next to the screw driver that had been used to free it from its place.

Ken went back to the living room and as he sat down he looked at his wife. Peaceful in her sleep, but he knew this was the last straw. Something had to be done to help her with her depression and her drinking. Maybe Doctor Pete could help him there too.

By now it was two-thirty and Ken took the afghan from the couch and put it over his wife. He bent down and kissed her forehead. *We'll get this fixed, honey,* he thought.

CHAPTER 16

Clyde was at work this afternoon. Seems his job had evolved into filling the pickup truck with the pile of dirt and roots and rocks and stuff, and taking it to the other side of the island where they were filling in a swampy area. There he unloaded the pile from the truck into a bigger pile by the edge of the water, and eventually a big tractor with a front-end loader would come and put it into the muddy, foul smelling, large swampy lot. The plan was to fill it in with dirt and they'd already blocked off the source of the water, they thought, so that would handle the problem of this in the long run. Clyde doubted they'd fixed the problem but that wasn't his to worry about, so he just did what he was told and left to get another load. As he was leaving the pond he thought he saw Eddy's truck, the guy he was supposed to meet up with when he came back to the island. The guy was driving away and didn't seem to see Clyde, or maybe didn't want to see him.

As Clyde drove his pickup up the driveway to the street, he again thought he saw Eddy's truck at the next corner, so he decided to see if he could get his attention and talk about the things on his mind, like where had Eddy been and what was he doing, and weren't they supposed to meet-up a couple of days ago, and where was his money?

The truck with Eddy turned the corner and so did Clyde. He was sure it was his supposed-to-be buddy now. Finally, Eddy got to the end of the street and turned into the ferry line. The line was moving onto the ferry and Clyde couldn't follow so maybe Eddy hadn't seen him. At least Clyde hoped that's what it was.

If Eddy was avoiding him, then maybe it was time for Clyde to leave the island too. He needed to think this through, and really decide what was best for him. If Eddy left, would he be back? Was Eddy even worried that Clyde might be in trouble?

CHAPTER 17

Eddy had seen Clyde but now wasn't the time for them to meet-up. Eddy was on his way to Seattle to visit the free-health-clinic. That itch in his groin had become really red and now was not only an itch, but a pain. An all-the-time pain. He was pretty sure who he'd caught this from but now the problem was how to get rid of it.

Seeing Clyde also brought back the problem of Becky. Did Clyde stick around long enough to see him finish up with her? Now Eddy was thinking maybe he did need to get with Clyde and figure out what should be done if Clyde had seen the end of the deal. Or should he just keep going after his doctor appointment in Seattle? Eddy decided he'd think about that after his pecker problem was fixed.

CHAPTER 18

Dr. Pete was in his office when Ken got there. St. Joseph Retirement home was always a busy place. Today a van was parked in front of the office doors and about fifteen people were either getting on it or were already seated inside of it.

Ken went in to find Dr. Pete in his office but a resident was in there with him. Ken could hear the conversation as he waited outside the door.

"...and after we see the museum we will have an early dinner at the Fish House on the water front, then we will be back. Didn't you get the flyer explaining all of that?" It was Natalie Ann Greene doing the explaining and being exasperated.

"Yes, I know all of that. Sister Nora just wanted me to find out what time you expect to be back here. Would you say seven or later?" Dr. Pete was talking in his calm-the-patient-down voice.

"The van will pick us up at seven so I expect it will be closer to eight when we get back here. Now I must go. We have a ferry to catch to get there you know." And Natalie came out of the office and hurried past Ken and out the door and into the waiting van.

As Ken went into Dr. Pete's office he could see the frustration on the doctor's face. "Dealing with her is like talking to a wall sometimes. Glad I'm not on this trip with her in charge, but hello Ken. What can I do for you today?"

Ken sat down on the chair in front of the desk and said, "I'm glad I don't have to deal with her either." He shifted in his chair then said, "Just came to ask if you knew the family of Becky Coop?"

"Yea, knew the Father. Nice guy but really hen-pecked. When his wife started into menopause she became really a shrew and made him pack up and move to Alabama where she was from. He had to leave his boat and camper and his truck. A buddy of his sold all of them for him and when they moved, they left their daughter here too. She didn't want to go so they left and she didn't. I think she lives in Seattle now."

"Did you hear about the golf course body we found?" Ken was making notes. Didn't want to forget any of this info.

"Who hasn't? Did you find out who it was or who did it?" Now Dr. Pete was interested too. He'd heard lots of speculation amongst the residents from

St. Joe's that frequented Murph's Place. *Be good to hear some facts*, he thought.

Ken looked up from his notebook. "This is what I know so far. The lady was Becky Coop. She died of strangulation. She was a party-girl living in Seattle. Don't know why she was here, nor do we know who she was with. We think she is around thirty-something. Do you know any more about her or where he family is so we can contact them?"

"No. Never heard from either of them after they moved. I did hear that Becky was living in a big house on Queen Anne Hill. Some place that takes in nearly homeless women. Don't know the name or exactly where it is but if it's the one I do know about, it houses prostitutes. I'll find the address for you or maybe Murph knows better where it is. Been in this business since 1920 something I heard," said Dr. Pete.

Ken said, "Good idea to ask Murph. Can you think of anyone here on the island that might know where the Coop family is now?"

After smoothing his hair, Dr. Pete moved his hand back down to lay on the desk. "No, not really. The wife was always a weird duck and the husband worked on a fishing boat so was gone lots of the time. Never did know who the guy was that sold the boat and stuff. Sad, this happening here on the island. The Coop family were not really very social. I think I saw them once at a Music in the Park event but that's all I remember. Becky was little then. A lot younger than my kids so we didn't really interact during any of our summers that we lived here. Sorry I can't help more."

"You've helped me more than I expected. Thanks Pete." Then as he stood up to go he said, "Going to the party at the Mansion next week?" The mansion was owned by Haven Port Island's Richard Reinholdt, as near to royalty as the island could claim. The Reinholdt family had lived here for over one hundred years and Richard was the last of the clan. He loved to entertain and since his nephew, a well-known pianist had his car accident and moved in with him, they hosted musical dinner parties quite often and invited many of the town's people to join them.

"Oh yes. Are you?" Pete was aware of Ken's wife's problem with booze, but didn't ask about her.

"Not sure. Maybe not. And that's something I'd like to ask you about." Ken sat down again and spent the next hour discussing with Dr. Pete the available services on the island for helping his wife with her depression and drinking problem, and before they finished, Dr. Pete had written down a name and phone number of someone he thought was a good place to start.

Ken left after thanking Dr. Pete profusely, and feeling his meeting with Dr. Pete was a huge success, in more ways than one.

CHAPTER 19

Ken and Murph and Dr. Pete might have been happy with how this day had turned out but Clyde wasn't. He knew he had one more day of work and that Daryl said he could stay with him as long as he needed to, but how was he going to find Eddy and get that problem off his mind? Eddy owed him $200 and said he'd get it for Clyde the next day after their original meeting. They'd made a new plan that Clyde would come back over to the island the next day after the party night at the golf course that Eddy arranged, and Eddy would give him the money and they would be square. Several weeks ago Eddy was living in Seattle where Clyde usually crashed. It was down by the water front in a building that had been converted for homeless men to stay. They had showers, and a laundry facility and you had to be on a waiting list to be allowed in. Eddy was there when

Clyde finally got admitted. At the time Clyde was working at a restaurant on First Avenue as a dishwasher and was making pretty good money. Well, pretty good for him. He worked from six in the evening until closing, which was only seven hours, and got paid every week. He was saving his money so maybe he could get an apartment, and he had a little over $250 when Eddy asked him for a loan. Eddy would get his paycheck next Wednesday but he needed to pay his kids day-care by this Friday so, after sharing a bottle of rum, Clyde believed him and gave him the money. That's why Clyde had come over to the island to meet up with Eddy, and Eddy had arranged for this party-time at the golf course, but Eddy also had a plan. First he did his thing with Becky, then Clyde did his thing but got a little carried away and decided it would add to his pleasure to cut off Becky's nipples. He pulled out his Xacto knife from his shirt pocket but Eddy stopped him before he got to the second one. She was screaming, so they stuffed her mouth with Clyde's handkerchief and Eddy told Clyde to get lost and he'd finish up here. As Clyde was pulling up his pants he said, "Where's the money?"

Eddy said, "Just get lost now but come back over tomorrow and I'll give it to you."

Clyde was just high enough on the weed that Eddy had given him to smoke, that he didn't think it through, just put the nipple in his pants pocket, finished dressing and headed for the ferry.

Now Clyde was worried. He'd heard of the girl's death so what if he couldn't find Eddy and get his money back? What if they found out he was part of the 'party' on the golf course? What if Eddy never returned the money? What if they blamed him for her death? Yes, maybe it was time for him to disappear but he really needed to wait for the money he'd get paid on Friday. *What a stupid place I've gotten myself into. It's time for me to leave too, as soon as I get paid.*

CHAPTER 20

Today was Friday. Payday for Clyde, and he was happy. Today he would go back to Seattle and maybe move down to Portland. He'd been thinking about this all night. He had an old Aunt that lived in the Portland area so maybe he would go there and crash. That is if she'd let him. He remembered his Mother talking about all the money her older sister had, so she probably had a big house and maybe his problems, for the rest of his life, would be over. Maybe.

At four-thirty the whole crew that was working on this construction site gathered by the trailer where the boss had his office. He came out with a hand full of envelopes and started calling names. When he got to Clyde he said, "Your envelope is short of the forty I gave you. Okay?"

Clyde just took the envelope and said, "Yes. Thank you."

"Are you coming back to work on Monday?"

"Not sure if I'll still be here but I will if I am. Is that okay?" Clyde was smiling. Now he had two opportunities presenting themselves. Portland and staying.

"Sure. If you show up, you have a job."

Clyde moved away from the group and opened his pay envelope. It held more than he'd expected by about eighty dollars, but he wasn't going to mention it. He needed all of this money so he could make a new definite plan.

CHAPTER 21

Old Fat Clem, as he was called by the locals, was as close as it came to Haven Port Island's resident homeless man. He did have a house but it had no furniture except for a couch that made into a bed and an old TV that sometimes worked. Someone had given the couch to him after his wife moved out and took all the household goods, including most of the furniture. She'd only left the kitchen table and chairs, and the little bedroom TV that was on its last legs she thought, but Clem still had it running most of the time.

Someone else had given him some pans to cook with and, because of his Social Security check every month, he was able to buy some food, and he could scrounge up more food from the restaurants at night. Sometimes he got the butt of a prime-rib, or sometimes just leftover baked potatoes, or part of a pie, but whatever it was, he was happy to take it off their hands, or out of the garbage if he got there after closing time.

His house was located just across from the corner of the golf course and he'd seen the two guys and a girl during their activities. Not all of it but some. He'd fallen asleep before she started screaming and then he had to go relieve himself again and when he remembered to go back to his viewing point, both guys were gone and he decided to just go to bed too. He had recognized one of the guys as Eddy who he saw sometimes looking in the garbage too, but didn't know his last name.

It wasn't until last night he'd heard about the body being found at the sand trap on that corner of the golf course. He thought maybe he should tell someone what he'd seen, then decided not to. It would take up too much of his time and he just didn't want to be involved. And after all, he was almost eighty-seven and too old to be of any use to the police.

CHAPTER 22

It was late in the day, almost five-thirty, and the Seattle FBI friend was on the phone with Ken again. "We found information on the two guys from the ID necklaces. Both are dead but would be in their nineties if still alive. One was from California and one was an uncle of a family that lived in Seattle and had a summer place at Haven Port. Turns out his wife was a relative of the Cousteau family from there. She'd married one of the military guys but neither of them are alive now."

Ken was really interested about this news. Clyde Cousteau was back on the island, and now a connection to someone here and someone he knew, and maybe he could find. When he got off the phone he finished making his notes then decided to go over to the bar by the marina. Maybe someone there would know where Clyde was living. At least Ken was hopeful and was chiding himself again for not checking that place before now.

It was five-thirty at the Marina Bar, as the local folks called it. The main room was just starting to get busy. The so called working man's crowd was filling the chairs at the tables and at the bar, but Sheriff Ken's appearance brought them all to attention and most were wondering who was in trouble now, and hoping it wasn't them.

Clyde and Daryl were in the truck and heading for their regular place, but Clyde barely talked on the way. He was busy making plans. When they got to the bar parking lot they both made remarks about the sheriff's car in the parking lot.

"Any reason the sheriff would want to see you?" asked Daryl.

"Not that I know of," said Clyde. "But you never know." But he did have an idea. He knew the Sheriff and Murph were friends, and Murph had seen him at the vacant house sleeping and ... *Tonight might not be a good time to see the Sheriff again.*

CHAPTER 23

Ken didn't have a picture of Clyde, but he sat down at the bar and started talking to the bartender at the bar. "Do you know Clyde Cousteau? I think he comes in here when he's on the island."

The bartender hadn't been raised on the island but he was sure Clyde had been in the last few nights. "Don't know him but a guy that people called Clyde has been here. Ask Tina. That girl sitting at that table over there. The one with the red hair. She was dancing with him."

Ken started over to the table of girls and two of them, including the red head, got up and went to the lady's room. He just smiled to himself and decided he'd still be here when they came out. The only one left at the table was a blond with a ponytail. She was not only overweight, but her clothes were so tight they left little to the imagination as to what undergarments were or were not present. He stood by the table and said, "May I sit down?"

"Sure," she said. "It's a free world, especially for cops."

He smiled and sat in the opposite chair. "I'm looking for a guy that comes in here named Clyde. Do you know him?"

"Of course. Everyone knows Clyde. Used to live here but now just here for work. He should be coming in any minute."

"Know where he works?"

"The construction job over by the high school."

"Thank you. You've been very helpful. You can tell your girlfriends it's time to come back to the table," and he got up and left the bar. Plan A was to go to the construction site tomorrow, then he remembered tomorrow was Saturday and he sure hoped they would be working on the week-end.

While Ken was talking to the pony-tailed girl, Clyde and Daryl had come into the bar. Clyde made a bee-line to the men's room and Daryl went to the table where his friends were already sitting. "Know why the sheriff's in here?" asked Daryl.

"Yea. He's asking around about Clyde. Must not have seen you guys come in."

"Yea. Must not have." The waitress was now at the table and Daryl ordered a beer and the other two guys ordered another one too. They didn't really care or wonder if Clyde was in trouble because it was Friday night and time to party.

Ken had seen what he thought was Clyde come in but couldn't see him when he got up to leave. Now Ken decided he'd go home, check on his wife then come back. Surely Clyde would have a drink before he left to do whatever. And he went out the door and drove away.

Clyde looked out of the men's room door and couldn't see the sheriff. He slowly walked over to the table where Daryl and the others were sitting and said, "You know, I don't feel too good. Okay if I just go sit in the truck and maybe take a nap?"

"Okay with me," said Daryl just as the waitress was back with their drinks and Clyde went toward the exit.

A beer did sound good but better safe than sorry he decided as he got into the truck and made himself comfortable. He'd have a beer later and maybe some food.

CHAPTER 24

When Ken got home his wife was in the kitchen and talking on the phone. "Okay honey. Looking forward to seeing you tomorrow.

As she hung up their house phone, Ken moved in and kissed her cheek. "Who was that?" he asked.

Phyllis smiled as she picked up her glass that was almost empty. "Colleen and Dick are coming for a visit tomorrow. They're on their way to Hawaii to celebrate their twentieth wedding anniversary but are stopping off here on Saturday and leaving Sunday to continue their trip. Their plane arrives at SeaTac around noon so they should be here about two. Will you be able to be home?" She was smiling and took another drink.

Ken said, "I'll make sure of it. Is the bedroom ready?"

"Should be. I got it ready for the next visit after the last one at Christmas." And she took another drink that emptied the glass.

"Let's go check it out," said Ken and took the glass out of hand and put it on the counter. "Then maybe we could go out for dinner if you feel up to it."

He took her hand and they both headed to the stairway. The bedroom was in perfect order for incoming guests. Clean sheets on the bed and the upstairs bathroom was ready too. Towels clean, a new bar of Ivory soap and a new roll of TP. As they walked down the stairs Ken said, "How about going to the restaurant up by the ferry. The one on the water?" Phyllis just nodded her head yes. And *they make good drinks,* she thought.

CHAPTER 25

Murph left his bar around quarter-to-seven. Bibb was there and seemed to have everything under control so he'd called Lisa to meet him for a late dinner. She was waiting for him by the door of the restaurant and as they walked in, Ken and Phyllis were just leaving.

Murph said, "Got time to have a drink with us before you leave?"

Phyllis immediately said, "Yes, but I'm full of coffee." She was smiling and took a quick look at Ken.

Murph was up to speed on Phyllis's problem and said, "Well, how about tea or …?"

They were all walking to a table as Phyllis answered, "No tea, but wine would be good."

Ken just smiled. They'd made it through dinner with no booze but one glass of wine should be okay.

The waiter was there with four menus and Ken

said, "We just finished eating but we'll have a glass of wine with our friends while they order."

Murph said, "Bring us a bottle of Merlot and we'll order after we've had some."

The waiter moved away to get the wine and realized he was still holding the menus. *Oh, well. I'll take them back when I deliver the wine."*

Ken was sitting facing the bar and saw Old Fat Clem come in and the bartender moved down to the end of the bar to talk to him. After a short conversation, the bartender left and went into the kitchen. He was back in a few minutes with a small cardboard box. He said something to Clem then handed the box to him. Clem nodded his head and took the box, then turned and left.

Murph had noticed this activity too and almost at the same time Murph and Ken looked at each other and started to say, "Wonder if he saw anything." Then they laughed because they knew that just because Old Clem lived that close to the golf course and had seen something at the sand trap, would he remember?

CHAPTER 26

The sheriff pulled into Clem's driveway the next day at eleven o'clock on this sunny morning. He'd waited until now because he was pretty sure Old Clem was not an early riser and he was right. Clem answered the door in his pajama bottoms topped by a red t-shirt, and he was bare footed.

"Mornin' Sheriff. Did I do something wrong?"

Ken smiled. "Not that I know of. Need to confess?"

"Come in. Might as well have coffee while we talk about it," said Clem and stepped back into the living room.

When Ken entered he could smell the coffee brewing and could see that Clem probably had slept on the make-into-a-bed couch. The TV was on and Clem moved to turn it off then motioned Ken to follow him into the kitchen area. "Come in here."

Clem led the way and again just motioned for Ken to sit at the able. He then filled two cups with the newly brewed coffee, took them to the table and sat down himself.

Ken was looking around. The sink was full of dirty dishes and he wondered who, if anyone, looked after this man. The floor certainly could use a good mopping and from what he'd seen of the living room, it could use some cleaning attention too. Well, it wasn't a problem he needed to address now so he just said thank you when the coffee was set in front of him.

Clem put both hands on the table and then slowly lowered himself into the chair. When he was settled Ken said, "Do you know about the body found at the golf course?"

Clem nodded yes.

"Did you notice any activity at the golf course lately that might be connected to that?"

Clem wiped his mouth with the back of his hand. "Well I did see two guys and a girl standing in that sand trap. They were just talking and after I went to pee I forgot to look again."

Ken was now paying even more attention. "Did you recognize any of them?"

"Well the girl has been there before. Sometimes brings dates there to have sex. Don't know her name. One of the guys was Eddy. I see him around but don't know where he lives."

"Do you see Eddy regularly somewhere?" asked Ken.

Clem wiped his mouth again after taking a drink of coffee. "Don't see him regularly anywhere. Just around. He gets old food from the restaurants like I do. Do you know about that?"

Ken did know that Murph's and a couple of other restaurants gave away food sometimes.

"Do you get this food together? From these restaurants I mean?"

"Sure. I'm not very rich and getting their leftovers at the end of the day is a good way to be sure I'll be eating something. Sometimes it's just left-over rolls but that's better than nothing."

Ken smiled. It would be better than nothing but what a way to live. "Do you need more help with the food situation? I could have someone come by and ..."

Clem sat up straighter. "No need for more help. I'm not a charity case yet. Don't send one of those nosey social workers over here. I'm doing okay as I am."

"Okay. I understand you want to be left alone. Just wanted to help."

"I know you meant no harm," said Clem. "But I want to be left alone."

Ken smiled at him. "Do you have anyone that checks on you?"

"*NO. I JUST WANT TO BE ALONE!*" Clem said

in a louder voice and then slowly stood up and went to open the kitchen door. "I think it's time you left if you have nothing else to ask me."

Ken stood up too and walked toward the door. "Sorry I upset you Clem. Let me know if you need anything, okay?" And he went out the door, around the house to his car, and backed out of the driveway. As he drove away he wasn't thinking about Clem, he was wondering how he'd find Eddy.

As he approached Murph's restaurant he decided to stop and have lunch. Maybe someone in there knew about this Eddy guy.

CHAPTER 27

Sitting at the bar at Murph's were the usual guys, Steve, George and Larry. Both Steve and Larry were busy telling George to buck-up. His girlfriend Pat Olson would be back from California soon. She'd gone to finish the sale of her condo and to bring back her belongings. Her friend Gail was with her and they would drive back together too, maybe with a truck full of stuff. The guys were reminding George that while the ladies were there in California, they would also try to sell some of the furniture. "After all, she wouldn't need all that stuff if she continues to live at St. Joseph's, but she'll need a bigger unit," said Steve.

"That's already been arranged," said George. She'd also told George that she knew exactly what furniture to bring. It was just all the rest of the stuff that she had to find a home for, and that might take a few days.

George was nodding and agreeing but he still missed her. When she got back he wanted to never let her leave him again. Now he was worried that if he asked her to marry him, would she say yes? She was pretty independent but he knew she liked his daughter and grandkids, and they liked her so... He decided he better try to stop worrying and took another drink of coffee, wishing it was something stronger to get him through this.

The Sheriff sat on the barstool next to Larry, and when the conversation between the men lagged, he said, "Anyone here know of a guy named Eddy that is sort of drifter and may be homeless?"

Murph moved down to where the guys were sitting. "I might. Old Clem and this younger guy sometimes come by the restaurant as we're closing, asking if there are any left-overs they could have. I think I heard Clem call him Eddy once. Is he a person of interest?"

Ken said, "Can I order some lunch first then I'll tell you what's going on."

"The usual?"

"Yes and coffee please." Ken was smiling and so was Murph as he went to the kitchen to place the order for a BLT and fries.

When Murph came from putting in the lunch order, Steve, Larry and George all turned in their seats to face Ken and waited for him to continue with whatever information he had.

"Well, I think I might have a lead on one of the guys that was in the sand trap the other day. We know who the girl was and I think we know one of the guys now, so I'm looking to talk to Eddy." The Sheriff turned to speak to Murph. "Do you know where he lives?"

"Except for here in the kitchen, I've only ever seen him in his truck," said Murph. "He drives an old pickup. It's a Ford. It's black, except for the streaks of rust on the doors and along the bed. It's about a 1980 model, short bed. Nothing to make it stand out anywhere. He might even be here tonight. We seem to be on his weekend stop. If so, I'll make sure to get more info."

Ken said, "I'm not aware of someone or anyone living in their cars or trucks but I'll start looking. There was a guy last year that was living in an RV but he moved on. Thanks Murph. That's a place to start." His lunch was ready for him and as Murph delivered it he said, "Let me know if you need more help," and he smiled at the Sheriff.

CHAPTER 28

Eddy was not far away from the golf course but it was too early to stop at Murph's or any restaurant for left-overs. He still had some pizza he'd gotten last night and he decided he'd go park down by the Marina Café and have lunch. The parking lot there was the busiest around and lots of pick-ups were owned by the guys that frequented this bar. He blended in pretty good and could sleep here until at least midnight, most nights. Then he would move to the underground parking at the mall and he could stay there until five in the morning when the first mall worker came in. After that he could park by the ferry or at the high school when it was in session. He had a pretty good plan going, and so far no one bothered him or even noticed his parking pattern. At the moment he was going to the ferry to go to Seattle and hoping not to run into Clyde. The two hundred dollars he'd borrowed was almost gone and Eddy was hoping to get a loan from another guy he knew in Seattle. There wasn't a plan to pay either of these loans back but if he got the money today he would be on his way to Montana and a job in the mines. It was time to get out of Haven Port and they'd never think to look for him there in the mines.

CHAPTER 29

The sheriff's car pulled out of Murph's and was headed home. His daughter was probably there by now and he sure wanted to see her.

When he pulled into his driveway he saw a light blue Chevy parked by the curb out front. *It must be their rental car,* he thought, and it was. As he got out of his squad car, his daughter Colleen came out of the door and was hugging him before he could get to the porch.

"Oh Daddy. I'm so glad you're home. Mom's ... well Mom is ....

"I'm so sorry you had to see her like this. She's been drinking hasn't she?"

Colleen was crying when she said, "Yes," but that's all she could manage to say.

Ken kept his arm around her shoulder as they walked into the front room.

Phyllis was sitting in her favorite chair. The lounge chair was fully extended with the foot rest up and the TV was on. Beside the chair was a bottle of vodka and a glass that had some of the liquor still in it. The ice cubes were mostly melted and she was asleep with her mouth wide open and snoring.

"I tried to wake her but she just mumbled and went back to sleep. I'm so glad you came home now. I was just about to call 911 and find you." Colleen used a hanky and wiped her tears and nose and was now standing by her husband. "Daddy, what can we do?"

Ken took Colleen's hand and started toward the kitchen. "Dick, come with us," he said. When they were all seated at the kitchen table he said, "I need to talk to you about this problem your Mother has."

Colleen nodded her head and Dick reached over and put his hand on top of hers. "What can we do to help," he said.

CHAPTER 30

Clyde was sort of at loose ends. He was alone because Daryl had left to go somewhere at seven this morning. Said he'd be home 'when you see me'.

Without a car and really no place to go, Clyde was sitting in the living room making plans. He'd decided he would leave today and go to his Aunt's house in Oregon. He was starting to realize that he wasn't going to get his money back from Eddy, and it was getting a little worrisome for him about the dead girl they'd found. The talk at the Marina bar was that the police were closing in on a person of interest, and that was enough to reinforce that now was the time to leave. He got up and went to the bedroom he'd been using. *Yep, it's time to leave and today is the right time.*

The backpack Clyde had would hold everything

he had here in the house, and he decided not to go back to the shelter where he'd been staying in Seattle. He hadn't left much there, only some sock and tee shirts and a pair of tennis shoes, and they weren't really worth the trouble of going back for, and besides, it would take time that he didn't feel he had.

With his backpack on his shoulder he went into the kitchen. By the phone was a pad and pencil, and he wrote a note to Daryl: "Guess I'll be moving on. Thanks for letting me stay here and getting me the job. Maybe I'll see you sometime in the future." And he signed it with a big capital C. He left the pad with the note still attached on the counter by the sink, and went out the back door. His plan was to take the ferry from here to Seattle, then a bus to Oregon. He was getting really anxious to get off the island and out of Washington.

CHAPTER 31

The Sheriff and his daughter and her husband talked for about an hour and had a plan too. Armed with the note Doctor Pete had given him, he called the number. It was a residence in Seattle and was only for women with drug or alcohol problems. A representative could meet with them at four o'clock today if they could make it to her office. Ken knew of this facility and he and his daughter Colleen decided what would happen next. She would stay with her Mother, and her husband Dick would go with Ken to the appointment. When the guys got home they would all sit down and discuss it with Phyllis. The plan would then be activated but Ken was worried about his wife's reaction to all of this. He hoped for cooperation but he was worried.

Dick and Ken left in the rental car and headed for the ferry. It was close to two-thirty and Ken was hoping to make the ferry that was supposed to leave at two-forty-five, and they did. This was a ferry ride that would take about thirty-minutes so they decided to get a cup of coffee from the upstairs restaurant. It wasn't really a restaurant but you could get coffee or beer or soft drinks and some food, like hot dogs, or donuts, or popcorn, or burritos, that they heated in the microwave. Ken wasn't hungry but Dick wanted a donut filled with lemon cream. That sounded so good to Ken he had one too. He was so happy to have someone whose opinion he valued with him to go to this meeting.

As the guys headed back down to the car Ken saw Clyde sitting toward the front of the boat. He really didn't have anything he could hold Clyde on, so he just made a note in his head to find out if he was still working at the construction site on Monday. That was pretty much all he could do now.

Dick noticed Ken's interest in Clyde and said, "One of your guys or part of a problem?"

Ken smiled and said, "If he's leaving town it might be a problem but I was told he had a construction job and the jobs not finished yet so I'll go check on him Monday. I have no real reason to retain him now but I guess he's part of a problem that I can't solve until Monday. Let's just go eat our donut and I'll worry about this later."

Dick took a bite of his donut and nodded

toward Ken. When he'd finished swallowing he said, "Sure wish I could do something to help you with this too."

The guys drove into the parking lot a little after three-thirty and found the office of their appointment meeting ten minutes before four o'clock. The receptionist picked up the phone and talked to someone then said to the men, "Dr. Wilson can see you now. Her last appointment ended early." She motioned them toward the door across from her desk that was her office.

Dr. Wilson was in her late fifties, with gray hair pulled up into a bun. She had bright blue eyes and a lovely smile that made the fellows feel they were in the right place. After introductions Ken explained his wife's problem and explaining where they lived, he told Dr. Wilson he felt it was because she never really settled into this new home and community. He didn't know why because all their other moves, even when their daughters were still at home, had been very successful. They met people and had friends and a good social life. He answered the Doctor's question about why they moved so much too: "I worked for the FBI and was transferred several times." Next question was "Were the daughters still at home?" Ken said, "No. They're both married and have families now. They live on the East Coast so we don't see them on a regular basis. I think that might be part of the problem too."

Dr. Wilson nodded. "Might be part of it. What are you looking for today?"

"Help to get her sober again and hoping she will be happy again."

Again Dr. Wilson nodded and said, "We can help her with that. Does she know you're here?"

Now it was Ken who said, "No. I left her with our daughter. She's been drinking today and was asleep when I left."

The meeting went on for about half an hour more and it was decided that on Monday Ken would bring Phyllis to this office and the three of them would discuss and decide what action was needed or should be taken. Dr. Wilson told Ken and Dick that usually patients at this facility took about two weeks to really work on the problem they had, then it took another few weeks for the problem to reach a point where it could become a non-problem when they went home.

Ken and Dick left Dr. Wilson's office with the plan they had hoped for. Phyllis would come to an appointment on Monday at ten o'clock. She would bring with her any medications she took on a regular basis, night wear, a bag with at least three changes of clothes, and hopefully the intent to stay as long as it took for her to put this problem behind her. Now all they had to do was go home and convince her this was necessary.

At the Sheriff's home, Colleen was busy

cleaning out the liquor cabinet. She'd found a wooden box in the garage and she was busy filling it. When she was done the only thing left on the shelves were a set of six shot glasses, all in different colors, six highball glasses and six wine glasses all with a gold rims, some plastic picks used for martini olives, and some stirring sticks for highball drinks. She carried the heavy box back to the garage and pushed it under the work bench. It wasn't hidden but would take some time to find if anyone was looking for it.

CHAPTER 32

Clyde had seen Ken on the ferry too, but was pretty sure Ken hadn't seen him. This just verified in his mind that he was doing the right thing. As soon as he got to Seattle, he walked up the hill from the ferry to the bus station, and paid for a ticket to go see his Mother's sister. As luck would have it, the next bus to Portland left in half an hour. He got himself a Coke and sandwich and chips to eat on the bus, and congratulated himself on his timing.

As he rode in the bus he was trying to remember his aunt's first name. His mother called her Sissy, but he was pretty sure her name was either Clara or Karen. He'd have to fake it until he found out. He had an envelope she'd written to his Mom but there was no name, just an address and it was tucked into his wallet. When he was getting dressed today he couldn't find the old dog tags he usually had in his jacket pocket but decided they would probably turn up in his back pack. For now, he was a happy guy traveling to this new adventure, and the itch in his groin only made him wish he'd remembered to take a shower before he left.

CHAPTER 33

When Ken and Dick got back to the house Phyllis was not only awake, but in the kitchen getting chicken ready to put into the oven for dinner. Colleen was sitting at the breakfast counter on a stool and was talking about their trip. "…and so we are going to our friend's condo and it won't cost us anything, really." She took a drink from her tea cup. "Just the plane ride and food and if we rent a car while we're there."

When the guys walked in, the ladies both went to their own husband and hugged them. "We're having a cup of tea. Do either of you want one?" asked Phyllis.

"Sounds good to me. How about you Dick?" replied Ken.

Dick said yes too, so Phyllis turned on the electric tea pot, got them cups and the tea bag holder that contained several choices. Ken chose Mint

Explosion and Dick took Black Tea with Orange. The teapot started to sing so Ken reached over, took it off its connection and poured boiling water in each of their cups. Colleen took her already wet tea bag off her saucer and put it back in her cup. She was ready for more water too but Phyllis said she was fine for the moment, "...but how about taking our cups into the other room. I'll be there as soon as I put this chicken in the oven."

Colleen and Dick and Ken all dunked their tea bags a few times then took them out of their cups, put them on the saucer in the middle of the counter, and headed for the living room. Phyllis put the pan holding the chicken into the already hot oven and picked up her cup. Then she went into the den and opened the liquor cupboard, intending to just add a little something to her cup and was startled to see it was empty of any bottles. When she saw that, she made an almost statement, "wha?" that Ken heard and went to see what had happened. He put his arm around Phyllis's waist. "Good idea to clean this cupboard out," he said and hugged her close to his side. Phyllis didn't say anything.

CHAPTER 34

Eddy's day wasn't going as well as Clyde's. As he pulled off the ferry in Seattle he got a flat tire. He pulled to the side and out of line looking for a place to park so he could change the tire. His jack was so old it broke as he started pumping the car up but a guy stopped and offered his jack. When the tire was finally replaced and the old one loaded into the back of his pickup he was back on his way to the clinic. First things first.

The clinic was located on what the locals called Pill Hill. Several hospitals occupied this hill along with the Free Clinic Eddy was headed for. He'd been there before but always at night. Here in the daytime and after he finally found a parking place, most of the seats in the waiting room were filled with those wanting to be seen. He checked in at the desk, then took a seat that had an old man on one side and a woman with a very small baby on the other. The baby was crying but not loud. The old man was drooling and whoever he was with kept reminding him to wipe his nose and mouth. The whole room was noisy and Eddy was already on edge from the flat tire incident so when a chair next to the door became vacant he moved. Now he only had a woman next to him. She was beautiful and smelled like lilacs and Eddy was happy, but it took almost an hour and a half before his name was called. *Finally,* he thought.

When he came out of the clinic he sure hoped the stuff they smeared on his private parts would start working soon. They'd given him two tubes of the stuff to use after he showered and washed his body thoroughly tomorrow and the next day. This made him smile when the doctor said it. His chance of having a shower today or tomorrow or even in the near future was between slim and none. *Oh well, things will work out. They always do.*

He got back to his truck and found a parking ticket on the windshield. He hadn't noticed that he'd parked with the back half of his truck blocking a fire hydrant. He pulled the ticket out from under the windshield wiper and got into the truck. He threw the ticket on the floor of the rider's side and started the truck. *What more can happen?* he thought as he pulled away from the curb. He was so busy fuming he really wasn't looking around at traffic and he ran into the rear-end of a police car.

Well, maybe I'll get a shower before I get out of jail, he thought. *Things do work out sometimes.*

The officer of the police car was walking toward the truck. Eddy got out and met him with his hand out. Time for some niceties and he put a smile on his face. "So sorry. My fault. What can I do to make this go away?"

"Please show me your driver's license, registration and insurance information," said the policeman, ignoring the pro-offered hand to shake. "Shouldn't take too much of your time."

But that was a problem. Eddy had the license and registration, but no insurance so he took out his wallet and started going through it like he was looking for something. He found the registration and driver's license and handed it over, but kept looking, presumably for the insurance proof.

The policeman took the cards and headed back to his patrol car. He got on the radio, spoke for a few seconds then listened. He got back out of the car and as he approached Eddy he said, "This registration is outdated and so is your driver's license. A tow truck is on its way to get your truck and now I'd like you to get into the squad car, back seat."

A tow truck was coming up the street as Eddy

turned and slammed the door of the truck and he moved toward the police car. *Well, now for sure I will get to take a shower,* he thought as he patted the medicine tubes in his pocket. *Not a total loss.*

CHAPTER 35

It was Monday in the late morning and Sheriff Ken was tired. Really his spirit was tired but it affected his whole body. His daughter Colleen and her husband left Haven Port Island on the 5:35 PM ferry on Sunday evening, going back to the airport and the plane that would take them on to Hawaii. Yesterday was still heavy on his mind. Dick had filled Colleen in on what happened in Seattle at the meeting with the doctor while Ken was in the kitchen with his wife. He didn't give her all the details but just the bones of the visit. When Ken brought Phyllis into the living room he was carrying her tea cup and set it down on the coffee table. "Well, now that we are all together, let's have a little conversation," he said and reached over and took his wife's hand.

The conversation started with Colleen saying,

"Mom. I love you but do you realize you have a problem?"

Colleen looked at her then looked at Ken. She picked up her cup, took a drink then said, "Yes. I think I do. How do you know about it?"

From here the conversation went from "... because when we got here you were asleep in your chair, booze in a glass and you didn't recognize me when I tried to wake you up." To ... "I'm so sorry I was taking a nap but ..." to finally these words from Ken, "I think I have a plan to help you fight this and get back to your old self."

It was almost midnight when they went to bed that night. All through dinner and afterwards Ken was explaining the program he wanted her to join, and Dick was offering some of his knowledge on how these programs worked and how well they worked with people willing to really try to follow the guidelines. Dick was a doctor in the Navy and he'd dealt with these kinds of problems many, many times.

Sunday morning Colleen was helping fix breakfast and the guys were sitting at the breakfast bar drinking coffee. Colleen put the breakfast sweet rolls into the oven to warm and Phyllis said, "You know what? I think going to that clinic for a few weeks makes sense. It's obvious to everyone, even me, that I've lost control and I'm not happy about that, so honey, the meeting on Monday will be the first day of my new and happy life."

Colleen was closest and stepped over and hugged her Mom. Dick was next and then Ken took her into his arms and said into her ear, "I love you so much for making this decision." Phyllis clung to him and said, "I love you too. That's the important part."

Now it was Monday and Ken was on his way back to Haven Port. It was almost noon when he got off the ferry and he decided lunch would be good. He'd only had coffee this morning and now he had new hope and he was trying to feel happy. Along with that came hunger. *Maybe I'll have breakfast for lunch*, he thought. Then he smiled. Been a long time since he'd done that but today was a new beginnings kind of day for him too.

As he entered Murph's bar he was smiling. "Hi. What's making you so happy?" asked Murph from behind the bar.

"Just getting home from taking Phyllis to the rehab Dr. Pete told me about. Not happy to be without her but happy that this step has been put into action," said Ken.

Murph smiled at Ken and went around the end of the bar and gave Ken a hug. The bar only had a few people in it and no one seemed to notice these good friends in an embrace. Ken really needed this and he was even smiling wider as they separated. "Thank you. I might be back for more hugs as the days go by."

"Any time my friend," said Murph. "This isn't an easy thing but you have friends to help see you through them." He gave Ken a bump on the arm with his fist and went back to behind the bar. "Coffee or lunch?" he said.

Ken sat down on a stool and said, "Is it too late for breakfast?"

Murph said, "No. Not for a friend. What do you want?"

And as Ken ordered, Murph filled a cup with coffee, then took the order to the kitchen.

Ken felt better now. He knew he'd done the right thing for Phyllis and he realized he had someone in his corner all the way on this move. A small part of the weight he was feeling seemed to lift. This was certainly doable for both him and Phyllis and then they could get on with their lives, and maybe be happy living here.

CHAPTER 36

When Ken got back to headquarters, he had a message waiting for him from Dr. Pete. "Call me please." As he dialed Dr. Pete's office number he wondered if this was another crisis or what.

"Hello. This is Dr. Pete."

"This is Ken. Got more problems for me to solve?"

"Not at the moment but I just got an email from Dr. Wilson thanking me for my referral to her place and she said your wife is lovely and being very cooperative."

Ken let out a sigh. "Thanks for that information. Yes, I took her there this morning and she has been in full agreement with what needs to be done. Got any idea on how long this treatment will take?"

Pete and Ken discussed what would be taking place. They talked about the meds they would give her to wean her off the desire and need to drink alcohol, and discussed the duration of treatment. When they were finished Ken almost hung up when Pete said, "Oh I almost forgot. Was talking to Curley about the body this morning. He said he told you they found two different semen samples, indicating two men had sex with her. Seems that one of the guys probably had a raging case of a venereal disease so the next guy may be infected too. Might be helpful if the guys are ever found."

CHAPTER 37

Ken was bored. He was home on this Monday evening. He'd had dinner of left over chicken made into a sandwich and a glass of milk. That part of his evening done it was still only seven o'clock. He went into the room they called an office and turned on the computer. *Maybe I'll catch up on my Solitaire playing,* he thought. First he opened email to see if there was anything new and found a message from his FBI contact in Settle. "You know we get regular reports from the local police on arrests and I always just cruise through it looking for a familiar name. Didn't find any name but what caught my eye was that one guy was in jail because of no insurance after an accident with a police car. What really got my attention was that he was from Haven Port. Got anyone named Eddy Hanson that you need to talk to that might be in a Seattle jail?"

The sheriff was certainly interested and emailed back asking for contact info, and almost immediately an answer came back with a phone number and name. *Bingo,* thought Ken, and reached for the phone.

After he identified himself he was transferred to the department he needed. Proof that the prisoner was still there, the fact that he wanted to visit this person and the address where Eddy was being held was given, and an arrangement for Ken to come identify him as a person-of-interest in a murder was established. He'd be in Seattle tomorrow at nine o'clock to get the necessary paperwork started. If possible he wanted to leave Eddy in the Seattle jail but he'd do whatever was necessary to keep him incarcerated. Next he emailed his FBI friend and thanked him for the info, and filled him in on the circumstances.

By now it was nine o'clock and Ken decided to turn in early. He was bone tired for some reason and he started up the stairs to the bedroom. After a shower he was in bed and decided he didn't need to turn on the TV. In a matter of minutes, he'd stretched out and made himself comfortable, and was asleep.

CHAPTER 38

Eddy was awake but not sitting up yet when a guy came by with something metal banging on the bars. "Up and at 'em!" he was yelling. Then he stopped at Eddy's cell and after banging on his bars said, "Get yourself up and dressed. You have a visitor."

Sure I do, thought Eddy but this was his first morning here so whatever they said is what he'd do. He'd had a shower last night and then slept in his shorts, and today he only had his old dirty clothes. Even he could smell the lived-in smell of his sweat shirt but this is what he had so he put it on, and as he was tying his tennis shoes the guard was back to take him upstairs.

Eddy finished his shoe tying, stood up and followed the guard. He thought maybe he was going to court but when they approached the visitor's area and he saw Sheriff Ken talking to the officer, his heart sank. This was not a good sign.

The guard took Eddy into a small windowed room and told him to sit down by the desk. As he sat down the guard went to the door and signaled to the officer behind the counter that they were there, and both the officer and Ken turned and looked across the hall, and at Eddy.

CHAPTER 39

D r. Pete decided he would treat himself today and go out to lunch at Murph's Place. It was a beautiful day so he just put on his jacket, stopped by the office to tell Sister Nora where he was going, and he headed out to walk the few blocks. It wasn't long before he opened the door to the bar, and walked in only to be confronted by the bar stools filled and most of the tables too.

"Hey Dr. Pete," said Murph from behind the bar. "Nice to see you."

Pete move over to the end of the bar and said, "I didn't think you'd be this busy today. What's going on?"

"Not sure but most of the ladies at the table are headed for the golf course to play a tournament. It starts at two o'clock so they'll be leaving soon."

"Well if you give me a menu and a cup of coffee

I'll perch at that table over there. Just wanted a little lunch and needed a walk so here I am."

"Glad you could come by. Go ahead and sit down and I'll bring your coffee over. Take anything in it?"

"Could use a little sweetener, please," said Pete, and moved toward the table just down from the door.

Murph filled a cup and picked up a spoon and the sugar and sweetener container. He also picked up a menu. As he was setting down the cup and other things, the Sheriff came in the door.

"Hey Ken. Welcome," said Murph.

Ken smiled and then noticed Dr. Pete at the nearby table. "Hi Murph. Coffee please and I think I'll sit with Pete."

Dr. Pete looked up and smiled too. "Yeah. Sit here with me."

Very soon the ladies at the tables began to leave. Three ladies were carrying their golf bags but now they were going to ride with someone else in a car. Golf bags got heavier and heavier as their shoulder got more and more tired they found. When the last lady left there was only Murph and Ken and Pete and one other guy still in the room.

"Gets quiet in here sometimes," said Murph and everyone laughed, even the guy at the bar.

Bibb, Murph's relief bartender, come in through the kitchen door. "Did I miss the rush today?"

he said.

Again everyone laughed and the guy at the bar said, "So every day you have a rush hour lunch?"

Murph said, "Well only when the golf course has an event. But we do okay crowd wise most lunch times."

The guy said, "Are you the owner?"

"Yes I am." And he walked behind the bar down to where the man was sitting.

"My name is Mac. Are you interested in a new cook or bartender?" And he was offering his hand to Murph.

"Hello. I'm Michael Murphy but most people call me Murph," and they shook hands. "What did you have in mind about being a cook or working here? Do you mean full time?"

Bibb was listening to this exchange of information too and hoping it wouldn't affect his status here.

Murph said, "Let's go into the restaurant and talk. Follow me," and both men went to the end of the bar and through the door that went past the kitchen and into the other side of the building into the eating area.

Bibb picked up the coffee pot and went to fill the cups of Pete and Ken. "You guys ordering or just drinking coffee?" he said as he poured.

Pete said, "I think I'll have a BLT."

Ken said, "Me too."
Bibb said, "Both want fries?"
They both answered yes at the same time.
"You got it," and Bibb went to put in the order.

CHAPTER 40

Half an hour later Murph came back into the bar and went to sit with Ken and Pete who were almost finished with their sandwiches.

"Selling the bar?" asked Ken.

"Nope. And not hiring new help either. That guy was an agent for bartenders and restaurant staff, including chefs, and was just making a stop at all the restaurant he sees. He's on his way to Tacoma but stopped here in Haven Port to see his brother who lives here. Mac is a brother of Fat Clem. Been trying to get him to move to Seattle but since he won't, they just stop by periodically to check on him. Clem won't take any money or anything from his younger brother so it's not ever a pleasant visit. I got his contact info in case Clem needs them or if something happens to him. Now, what's up with you guys. Got any more info about the lady that got killed?

Ken said, "Got a lead and maybe have the

person that committed this murder. He's in jail in Seattle for a traffic incident." Then he told both Murph and Dr. Pete how he happened to know this and about the visit this morning. "The most interesting thing today was that this Eddy has a Venereal disease which is the same one Curley told us about finding along with the seaman in the girl's body. We called the clinic this guy went too and got confirmation of the name and type."

Murph sat back in his chair. "Wow. You have found out a lot of stuff. Now what happens? Will you bring him over here to wait for trial?"

"Because we're part of King County, he'll stay there in the King County Jail until his trial comes up. We'll turn over all our evidence to the prosecutors over there and they'll take over. They'll file a felony murder charge against him and will authorize a warrant for his arrest. I went to the Seattle Jail and placed a detainer on Eddy so he won't be released and the rest will be taken care of in their court. We'll still be in the loop via email but unless they call any of us to testify, we are done with this." He took a drink of coffee. "I'm glad it's out of our hands. Now back to the every day stuff like where Mrs. Henry's cat is now; up a tree or asleep under her bed."

Murph smiled and Dr. Pete laughed out loud and then Ken laughed too. "So happy when all my problems have a happy ending."

Be Afraid

CHAPTER 1

The envelope was on the floor in the kitchen, by the back door. I picked it up and looked at the front but it was blank. It wasn't glued shut so I opened the flap and looked inside. The note said BE AFRAID. BE VERY AFRAID. That's all that was typed on the paper, but what was I supposed to be afraid of? I got over being scared of the dark many years ago but what was I expected to worry about now?

Tomorrow is my birthday so maybe it has to do with the surprise party that my fiancé Nancy is planning for tonight. I'm supposed to be at her house at six o'clock and we're going to the Golf Club for dinner. Yeah, that's probably it.

We got to the Clubhouse about six-forty-five and I could see some of my friend's cars in the parking lot but I didn't mention it. I didn't want to spoil things for her. Nancy said she wanted to eat in the side dining room because of the view of the mountain, and that was plausible because she's said that before, but as we entered a crowd of people yelled SURPRISE! and the party was on. This was one of the big birthdays for me. I was turning fifty, so when people got up to toast me, the jokes got pretty raunchy. They talked about how old I was turning tomorrow, and what I'd be missing in the bedroom from now on, and that I'd better start going to the gym more regularly. Well, I'm in pretty good shape because of my job, but I readily agreed. I just might start to slow down if I don't get into the exercise habit, so when Larry gave me the gift certificate to the Fitness Center I laughed, but was really glad to get it.

Larry is an old friend. When I graduated from the University of Washington and decided to join the Seattle Police Department, I was assigned to Larry as my first partner. He's about ten years older than I am, and he was a great trainer and mentor. When he retired from the department he went to work for the University, and now teaches Forensic Science there. I was made a detective a couple of years later, and I now live on an island across the bay from Seattle called Haven Port, but we see each other frequently, and he's still my mentor.

Someone brought a portable CD player to the party and so there was dancing and good food and lots of wine. It was a great party until it was time to open the gifts. I expected gag gifts and certainly got them: A baseball hat that said Antique Male, and a portable fold-up cane, and the Fitness Center gift certificate, and a bib that said Old Men Drool but the letters were all caps except for the d of drool so it read Old Men Rool. Funny stuff. Then I opened the cards and got more funny wishes and remarks about senility, and lots of how-to-age graciously suggestions. The last card I opened had just a folded up sheet of paper that said, AFRAID YET? Now that wasn't funny. I held up the note and asked who gave it to me? It was the same kind of envelope as the other note, and the front of the envelope was blank too. The message was typed just like the first one too, so no clues and no one there owned up to bringing it either. Now it's getting weird.

On the way home Nancy asked me about the note. I told her about the first one and said, "This isn't part of the birthday thing any more. I don't like being threatened."

"What can you do?" Nancy was starting to worry too.

"I'll take it to work and see if there's any clues the lab can find."

We were silent for a while but I was getting mad. "This isn't going to ruin my birthday celebration. Let's pretend it didn't happen."

"Okay," said Nancy. "I'll try."

I decided to change the topic by recapping the party. "Did you see Neil dancing? Bet his wife wishes he'd give it up." That made Nancy laugh.

"Hope her feet aren't too bruised. And why did he think he needed to yell and jump into the air?" She laughed again, then said, "And Paul sure can put away the booze. He drank almost the whole bottle of wine that was on his table and a couple of straight shots of bourbon, and then after dinner started drinking Grasshoppers. I don't even think he was staggering."

We talked more about the people at the party until we got to her house, and then we went upstairs and had our own party.

When I got home the next day, I decided to wash my car and generally get ready for next week. I like to do that on Saturdays. I was spraying the last suds off when my neighbor Hal came over. "Do you have to wash your buggy every week and show up us other guys?" He was smiling and he said this almost every time he came over, so I smiled too.

"Just a friendly reminder to all you slobs that don't mind dirty cars."

"Yeah, I know," he said. "Hey, have you seen any suspicious things happening around here?"

"No. Not really." I wondered why he asked.

"Well yesterday I saw a woman, at least I think it was a woman, coming from the back of your house, but it wasn't Nancy. I went out on the porch to ask if I could help but when they saw me they started to run down the street."

This got my attention. "What time was this?"

"Oh, I don't know, around four-thirty or five. I just got home from the dentist. Do you know who it was?"

"No, don't have a clue but thanks for the heads-up. What was the woman wearing?"

"A raincoat, and the hood was pulled up around her head. She also had on black rubber boots. That alone was sort of funny since it's been so sunny lately." So, clue number one. A runner in a raincoat.

"What color was the coat?"

"A light blue color but when she ran I could see the lining was a blue and red plaid. Does that give you a clue?"

"Nope. Just looking for details. If you see her again will you tell me, please?"

"Sure. Is something goin' on?"

"Hope not."

CHAPTER 2

Last night after the birthday party, I told Nancy I wanted to have this Saturday night alone. She is so kind and caring and she already understood why. On the evening of my birthday I've made it a practice to spend time at the cemetery with my parents. I was born at seven o'clock at night so I have a routine. I usually get to their graves around six-thirty, clean up around the head stones and tidy up the area, then I open a fifth of Black Label Jack Daniel's Bourbon, have a small swig, then pour the rest of the bottle around the head-stones. Before my Dad died he joked that what he was going to miss most when he was gone, was having a drink with me on my birthday, so I promised him I'd keep up the tradition. After he did pass away, Mom and I did follow the plan—took a drink then did the rest of the act together for six years until she died too. Now, the last four years, I've done it alone, but for both of them.

The notes were still on my mind but I decided I would not let it take over my life.

I spent Sunday with Nancy. She came over and I cooked outside. The steaks were good and so was the salad with apples that she brought over along with that crusty bread we both liked. Topped this off with a bottle of Merlot my co-workers gave me to help celebrate my 'this is a big one' birthday.

Nancy spent the night and we both left on the seven o'clock ferry on Monday morning to go to work in Seattle. Nancy is a lawyer and her office is in the down-town Seattle, walking distance from mine in the Municipal Building, so we get to have lunch together sometimes too.

I'd put both envelopes in a big baggy with a zip-lock since Larry and I were having lunch today. I needed to run this note stuff by him and maybe he could find something on the envelopes or message page that could help make an ID.

The envelopes weren't sealed so no saliva would be available for DNA, but I was hoping for finger prints or really, anything. Larry not only has access to the lab at school but also has one at home so when I gave this stuff to him, he said he'd give it the old college try.

Larry called me around four that afternoon.

"Found something that might be interesting. On one corner of the first envelope is a very small brown stain, and a partial finger print. In the second envelope, the paper with the message held another partial fingerprint but it didn't look like they came from the same person. The second one was definitely smaller in size and might be from a child," Larry said. "And the stain turned out to only be coffee."

Well, this was interesting but not exactly clues.

At about five-thirty I went down to the parking garage, ready to go home. Nancy and I wouldn't be together for a few more days since she was flying out to San Francisco early tomorrow for a trial she's been working on. Don't know exactly when she'll return but I already missed her. Maybe it's time we lived together, or even got married. I think I'll pursue this when she comes home. I'm tired of living alone.

On the way to the ferry to go home, I stopped for gas then decided to stop at Mickey's Pub for a beer. The parking lot was pretty full for a Monday but I guess there really is no preferred day to drink. Just recently Mickey decided to not allow smoking in the building but there was a covered patio in the back where you could still light up. Today had been warm and the evening was only a little cooler so the patio was packed with smokers and drinkers. Inside the AC was working and it was a lot quieter. Also, the air was nice and clean.

Mickey was behind the bar, not that it was unusual to see him there, but in the early evening he's usually in his office and sweet Alice, his wife, worked most nights until six, then she went home to their kids. These kids were in college but she still mothers them like toddlers.

I said hello as Mickey brought me a mug of beer.

A guy walked in a few seconds later and sat on a stool at the end of the bar. "Hi Mick. How's it goin'?"

"Pretty good. How are you tonight, Bob?"

"Okay I guess. Funny thing happened tonight. When I went out to my car after work I found a note on the windshield. On the front it said "Take this to Mickey's Pub. New advertising program?"

Now I was listening full bore and I didn't care if they noticed.

Mickey put his hand on the top of his bald head and said, "No. Nothing like that. Did it say anything else?"

"Yeah, when I unfolded it, it said, GIVE THIS TO THE SCARED GUY AT THE BAR."

Both Mickey and Jim looked at me since I was the only other one sitting there.

"Are you the scared guy?" asked Mickey.

I smiled and said, "No, not really," then I looked at Bob. "Where do you work?"

"About two blocks down at the boat repair. I

was going to stop here anyway but…"

Mickey had moved away to draw beers for the two new customers that had just come in and now was back in front of me. "What's going on? What's this scared stuff about?"

Mickey and I have known each other for many years. I was one of his first customers almost fifteen years ago and I knew he was concerned.

"Some jerk is trying to scare me by planting notes where I can find them." I looked at Jim again. "Would you give me the note?"

"Sure. Here." He handed it to Mickey, and Mickey gave it to me.

"Thanks." I put the note into my inside jacket pocket.

Mickey watched me do this and said, "Already got other notes?"

I smiled at him. He sounded worried so I wanted to ease his mind. "Got two so far and now this one. Don't know what it's all about."

"Maybe an old case?" Mickey was a retired policeman from Detroit so he knew there was more going on than I was saying.

"Might be, but I don't have a clue." I finished my beer and laid five dollars on the bar. "I'll have one more please." I smiled again and so did Mickey. We both knew there was no sense worrying until we had something to really worry about.

The next two days were uneventful as far as the notes were concerned. I had to go to court to testify on Tuesday, and Wednesday I taught a class on preserving evidence. I like to teach, and interacting with all the young law men. It gives me more energy too. Thursday I was back in court for the conclusion of the Tuesday trial. This perp was convicted of stalking and threatening a local politician who happened to be a woman I knew because of her work with law enforcement. Seems he thought she was targeting him with her anti-child abuse work and wanted her to stop. Of course she didn't, so he took it upon himself to try to convince her.

After the trial was over and because of the remark that Mickey made about it being an old case, I spent Thursday afternoon and Friday morning in the office at my computer, looking at past file cases. I started at five years ago. The cases I worked on that year were pretty much cut and dried. Bad guy caught, bad guy goes to jail and none of them were out on the streets yet. The next year was pretty much the same, but three years ago I got involved with a local gang member. It turned out he was a mafia wanna-be and was trying to infiltrate our detective's office. He applied for a job here in maintenance but because he had no work record, he was turned down. And, because I was present when he was rejected and I helped subdue him when he tried to climb over the desk to get to the HR guy, I thought maybe he was still a wacko out on the streets. That ended when I found a notice at the end of the file telling about his death that same year during a robbery.

Nothing else showed up that made me think this last note was connected to anyone in these files, so I looked back ten years. Still nothing. I'm beginning to get frustrated.

I confided my concerns about the notes to my Boss. He came up with a good idea. "Just let it sit until you can get a bead on this person. You aren't worth much to any one of us with this stewing on your brain. When you get hands-on info, you'll know what to do."

He was right. I should be working the case of the missing bank truck and I know my partner on this case wishes I would be working on it too, so back to business. The people I had on my list to talk to about this truck case live in a city North of Seattle. I spent the rest of Saturday in Everett and then spent most of Sunday in the office writing up my findings. I got home around five on Sunday night and I was actually expecting another note but there wasn't one. I ate cereal for dinner and went to bed around nine-thirty. I'd had enough of this week.

CHAPTER 3

It was Tuesday, and Nancy was due back at the airport at five o'clock. I picked her up and we went to her house, ordered pizza and generally renewed our friendship. The next morning, she was loading the washing machine and found another note. It said TELL FRAIDY CAT I'M STILL HERE. It really spooked her that someone had been in her house and it really pissed me off that this person would involve her. I called my office and arranged to have our lock expert come and change her front and back door locks and the garage door lock too. Then as we were leaving for our respective offices, I told Nancy I thought it might be time for her to move in with me. She just smiled and said we'd talk about it tonight. At least she didn't say no and I smiled all the way to work.

Now, this is Friday and I have to get my annual

physical at ten-o'clock. As I said before I'm in pretty good shape from all the moving stuff around, and I even get into a bad-guy chases sometimes. The doctor confirmed I'm still six feet one and one-hundred-eighty-two pounds. My BP is normal and I gave them some blood so they can check on cholesterol and other stuff. Then, after I got interviewed by the shrink, they printed out a report on my state of health. I signed on the bottom to show I'd received it, and they gave me a copy to take back to my office. Yes, sir. Harry Andrews is in good health and a stable state of mind, and I have proof.

I left the medical center and decided I wanted to celebrate so pulled out my cell phone and called Nancy. She was free for lunch so I drove over and she was waiting at the curb. We decided to go to the Inn At The Park, so in fifteen minutes we were sitting on the patio, sipping raspberry iced tea, enjoying the lovely day and each other. While we were waiting for our lunch, we watched as an elderly man and a younger woman came in.

Nancy smiled. "Isn't it nice when family can get together?"

I smiled too. "What do you mean family ... oh, as in husband and bimbo wife?"

"You have such a dirty mind," she said as she squeezed my hand, but she was still smiling.

They sat in the shade, in a booth by the wall

that had an umbrella. The woman dutifully took his cane and put it on the empty chair, then sat down next to him on the padded seat. We were still watching as he put his hand on her knee and moved it upward under her skirt.

I just grinned at Nancy and she made a face at me.

"Smarty pants. How did you know?"

"That's a retired Air Force General that I met once on a case. He's only sixty-something but was in a bad plane crash so that's why he walks like that and looks so decrepit."

"Well, good on him. Hope she brings him joy."

I wished that for him too but our food came and I no longer cared about his life.

Nancy came over for dinner that night and we ordered in Chinese. We were almost finished eating when I said, "Is now a good time to talk about you moving in here?"

"Well, I've been thinking about it and yes, I think you're ready for a daily keeper. I've already told my landlords I'll be moving, so now we need to set a date." She was smiling and of course, so was I.

CHAPTER 4

I keep my dark brown hair cut in a short crew-cut and so far, knock wood, I still have plenty of it, both on my head and chest and all the places I'm supposed to have hair. I've had a beard for an undercover thing. After that case I shaved it off but just kept the moustache. I got tired of that too, so now I'm clean-shaven, and since then, Nancy told she prefers me not to have facial hair. That was a big consideration too. I mentioned this because tonight there were two long black hairs in my bathroom sink by the master bedroom. I know they weren't from Nancy's short blond hair-do, and they weren't mine, but how did they get there?

I picked them up with a piece of TP and took them to the kitchen to find a plastic sandwich bag, the kind with a zip lock. Tomorrow I'd visit Larry again. I hoped he wouldn't be too busy to get on this right away.

I got lucky. Larry was able to start checking the hairs immediately and in an hour he called me. He said these hairs were probably Caucasian but didn't have a root on them for DNA, and they were probably from a male since he couldn't find shampoo residue, only soap, and to be more specific, the soap was possibly Ivory. So assuming this was a male and the hairs were not pulled out of a head but cut, why were they there? Well, I knew it was to scare me, but of what significance would these hairs be?

I had lunch with my Boss and I told him about the latest finds. He said, "Remember that case a few years ago where the guy cut off a lock of hair from his victims? Look him up and see what he's up to now.

After lunch I got on the computer and tracked him down. This was a man that had a hair fetish and when he went on trial, he said "I didn't mean to hurt the pretty ladies, I just wanted some of their hair for my collection and they wouldn't give it to me." I found his record and the report said he was no longer in jail and was living in Florida. In his file that followed him to Florida I found out he's in a 'home for disturbed seniors" that the Florida prison system runs. He was under twenty-four hour-watch and hasn't been out of his room alone for the last eighteen-months. Another dead end.

CHAPTER 5

George Thistle turned around to see who was talking. It was that loud mouthed guy in the corner who was always talking on his phone but didn't seem to realize how loud he was. Everyone around him knew he was talking to his son and wasn't happy with the way the son was responding. His usual phone conversation.

This bar where Thistle sometimes used as an office was not in the best part of Seattle, but not the worst part either. It was next door to a big chain grocery store and there was a hardware store on the other side. It was in a real middle-class strip mall. There was also a drug store, a UPS store, a shoe store, and a couple of other places like a laundromat and a barber shop. It was just a block off of a major street and not really in a neighborhood, but close enough so it was a busy place. Several people sat at tables here in the Pickle Bar, with their laptops open and spending this morning being busy doing whatever they did in this noisy place.

George Thistle looked again at the guy talking so loud, and decided he had better things to do than be upset with this jerk, and it was time to send another note to Harry. It had been three days since the last one and *we wouldn't want him to get too complacent.* He typed BEING AFRAID CAN DAMAGE YOUR HEALTH. He'd print this out when he got back to the portable printer he kept in the van he drove. Then, with a smile, he decided he'd leave it under Harry's windshield wiper himself, instead of the guy he'd hired to do the note deliveries. Just getting ready to drop another note made George very excited. The plan was working just the way it was intended.

He had another cup of coffee with cream and sugar, and although it wasn't even noon yet, he decided to have a shot of rum in it. A perfect drink for this rainy, very cool morning, then he started to think about the ending. He loved the ending that would happen soon, after a little bit more of the plan.

Although it had stopped raining and the sun was out, it wasn't very warm yet. When George got into the van, he started the engine and turned on the heat, and plugged his cell phone into the printer. He then put on the rubber gloves he had on the seat behind the equipment on the passenger's seat. While the printer spit out the message, he got an envelope out of the box he also had stored by the printer. As he folded and stuffed the note into the envelope, he smiled and thought *No finger prints for you this time Harry.*

Finding the entrance to the garage in Harry's downtown building in Seattle wasn't hard but he was afraid that finding the right car was going to be a challenge. Harry wasn't a creature of habit so he didn't park in the same place every time. Thistle drove around the first floor then the second floor of the parking garage, then got lucky. Just off the ramp to the third floor sat Harry's Subaru. Thistle noted the license plate number was right and stopped behind the dark gray car.

Thistle was a large man. Not really tall at five foot nine, but he had a large stomach and rear end, and that made him look large. He got out of his van and before he put the envelope under the wiper, he used a paper towel to rub the moisture off of the window. Then he crawled back into his van, took off the gloves and drove to the exit. It cost him two dollars to depart from the garage but it was worth it. Now he could make and send his report and get back to his own work schedule as a Private Eye.

CHAPTER 6

Today Nancy was free for lunch but not until one-thirty. We decided to just walk down to the water front and have a hamburger. This afternoon was sunny and almost too warm with no rain or even clouds like the morning had been. During my commute time this morning the weather was a whole opposite story, so we were enjoying this change. Seattle weather can change in almost a blink of an eye and today was proof.

We ordered our sandwiches and sat down at an outdoor table to wait. The view from this eating section was of the ferry dock and as we sat down a boat was just taking off for Bremerton, a small Navy military town just across the bay from down-town Seattle. As we watched its slow departure my attention was drawn to a couple of guys standing in the ferry parking lot. When we sat down, one guy had been pointing up to the restaurant where we were about to sit, and the other was busy being mad at the first guy.

The fat one kept motioning up towards us but I figured it was only that, a gesture up the hill. I noticed Nancy was watching them too but as I reached over to take her hand, she turned and smiled at me and at that moment our lunch was set on our table.

CHAPTER 7

If Harry could have heard the conversation of the two men, he still wouldn't have had any information that he would think he should act on.

The skinny guy gestured again with both hands but in frustration, and not really toward anyone. "There he is. Still just having lunch and doesn't seem concerned to be out in public." Then he looked up the hill and saw Harry put his hand on Nancy's and then he was giving her a soft kiss on the cheek. This made him even madder. "He's even kissing her. This has to stop! If you can't handle it pretty soon, I'll find someone who can!" As he said this last sentence he was poking the fat guy in the chest, then he turned and walked out of Harry's view.

The fat guy was not leaving yet but he moved closer to the stairs and out of Harry's sight too. George

Thistle had followed Harry from his office and then here to lunch. It was hard to follow people that were walking so slowly and not become apparent, but they didn't look around and George was being very careful, and trying to be as invisible as possible for a fat guy.

Thistle wished he could be eating with his prey, but as they got up to leave he came out of the men's restroom where he'd been lurking and he followed Harry back to work. Now he could go back to Haven Port Island and wait for Harry to come home tonight. And oh yes, have lunch too.

On the ferry Thistle opened his McDonald's sack and feasted on two Big Macs and Fries while he inhaled his chocolate McFlurry. It wasn't really enough for lunch but he had plans for an early dinner somewhere. Maybe at the Haven Port Mall. He loved their choices of food stalls and he started to plan which ones he would visit when he got there.

CHAPTER 8

During lunch today Nancy and I discussed when she would move in. She'd been packing and we'd already discussed what furniture she would bring. Her bed was smaller than mine, so she'd get rid of that. She had two green chairs that had foot rests. We enjoyed using them at her house when we watched TV and she would bring these. We also decided that anything that didn't fit into my house immediately could live in the garage until we made a decision about it. This included the coffee table that had drawers in it to hold books while they were being read. I already had a table in front of my chairs in the living room that was round and held all my magazines. I was hoping we wouldn't have a big conversation about this but until we did, her table was garage bound.

She'd contacted a moving company to come on Saturday and then we'd be living here together. I'm really excited and I'm pretty sure she is too. I promised her that this week I would clean out half the closet for her to use but what she doesn't know is that I'm going to move all my closet stuff in the extra bedroom, and she can have the walk-in in the master bedroom for her things. I know she'll like that.

When I got home I dropped my keys in the bowl on the divider between the kitchen and dining room and went upstairs to the bedrooms. An envelope was taped on the closet door.

I grabbed it and inside was the typical note that said, "DON'T GET TO PLACID. BE AFRAID. BE VERY AFRAID." Two notes in one day.

I looked around and could see the door to the balcony outside my bedroom wasn't closed completely. I moved over to it and with my arm, pushed it open. Outside was a ladder leaning up against one side, and so now I knew how the message leaver got in. I pulled out my cell phone and called our local Sheriff's office. When I explained someone had broken into my house, the Sheriff said he'd be right over with a finger print set and warned me not to touch anything. Yeah, like I would.

Sheriff Ken is an old friend and was there in about ten minutes. After we checked around the balcony door and the closet, we knew there were no strange finger prints. In fact, there were no prints at all. The perp had wiped it clean with a sterile wipe that he'd left in the waste basket in the bathroom. I had clean doors but not exactly what I wanted.

The Sheriff was also curious about the note. He read it then said, "What's that mean?" he asked.

"Not sure but I'm really getting tired of these. And I'll check with the neighbors to see if they saw anyone around my house today. The lady next door seems to know everything that happens." I was hoping it was the same woman/man that had been here before.

I told Ken about the other notes and the contents, and that I'd had my ex-partner checking them for prints.

"Okay. Glad you're on top of it," he said. "Let me know what you find out from the neighbors, okay?"

I was hoping against hope to have something to report to him as I ushered him out. I stood on the porch as he got into his car and left, then I turned and locked the front door and went over to talk to Mrs. Wallace. I think I woke her up because when she answered the door she was shoeless and yawning widely.

"Hello," I said. "Would you have a few minutes to talk to me?"

She looked up at me again and then I saw recognition come across her face. "Want to come in?"

she asked.

"Well, let me ask you a question and you can tell me if it will take a while to answer me."

I told her my house had been broken into today and I wondered if she'd seen anything.

"You better come in," she said and I followed her into the living room.

Turns out she was on her back porch when a thin guy came around the corner carrying a ladder over at my house. It was around two this afternoon. Since she was sitting in the shade he didn't seem to see her. She watched as he put the ladder up to the upstairs balcony, crawled up the ladder and in just a few minutes came back down. "I started to sneeze. I have allergies sometimes, and he heard me." He just walked around to the other side of the house and left."

"Did he run?"

"No, just walked pretty fast."

"What was he wearing?"

Sounded like the same guy as before to me. He was wearing a blue raincoat with a hood and she did notice the inside lining was red and blue plaid.

"It was a guy but I sort of laughed to myself that he was wearing a woman's coat. At least it looked like a woman's from here." Mrs. Wallace was smiling at the memory. "I thought maybe he was here to do some repairs but now that I think about it, it was very suspicious. I should have called 911. Sorry I didn't."

She put her hand on my arm and was looking sad.

"You didn't do anything wrong. You had no way of knowing," I said.

"Let me know if I can help in any way more," she said as I left, and I was thinking *sure wish you had called 911.*

I went across the lawn and looked at the ladder. It was mine. I could tell by the paint I'd dripped on the steps when I painted the garage door. I'd just stored it beside the garage a few months ago. Never even thought it might be used by an invader. Not in this neighborhood.

When I got back in the house I called the sheriff's office and left a message for Ken to call me. Couldn't hurt to get this guy and the ladder on his report too.

CHAPTER 9

Today is Saturday and moving day. Even though I'd found another note under my windshield, then the one in the bedroom, I decided not to mention it to Nancy. I'll worry about this alone as long as I can.

I'd spent last night at her house, and we got up at six-thirty. Per Nancy's instructions we stripped the bed and put the bedding, blanket and all the sheets and pillow cases, in the washer. Later she would transfer it to the dryer and it would be one more chore done. The pillows were already in black plastic garbage bags ready to move.

Nancy was in charge today. She is very organized and I knew she'd have a plan. All the boxes were labeled with a big red marking pen letter. L for living room, B for bedroom, G for garage, and after we'd had coffee, she washed and dried the pot and cups and put them into a box marked with a K for kitchen. She was bringing most of her dishes and cooking pots and pans because she had stuff I didn't. Like the pan for meat loaf and an angel food cake pan. Who knew we needed these?

At eight o'clock the moving truck and guys pulled up into the driveway and moving day began.

By two o'clock they were done unloading the truck and they left. Nancy looked at me and said, "Got any beer? Doesn't that sound good?"

It did sound good, and since we hadn't had breakfast or even lunch, I stopped by the phone and called our local pizza delivery, ordered, then went for the drinks. By the time the pizza was delivered we were on our second beer and really dug into the food. So far it had been a good day but it wasn't over. Now came the unpacking and other fun stuff like getting rid of the boxes and all the paper she'd used for the padding of the breakables. By seven o'clock we'd eaten the rest of the pizza and we were both pretty tired and decided to call it a day. Sitting in Nancy's chairs she'd brought over, we settled down to watch TV and at eight-thirty we showered and went to bed. Tomorrow would be another work day and we'd be ready.

CHAPTER 10

Sunday was more of the same at my house. Nancy was in the bedroom putting away clothes and moving stuff around to fit her way of thinking. I didn't care. I was so happy to have her here and with me, and I was happy to be doing the garage stuff. If I put all the boxes on one side of the garage, we could at least get one car in the garage at night. I thought I'd told the moving guys where to put them but somehow lots of the stuff got put near the entrance and had to be relocated. A good job for me.

On a few of the boxes Nancy had written BOOKS in red. I set all eight of these on the work bench. Wouldn't want any moisture to get into them. Then I restacked the rest of the boxes and went to find Nancy.

She was sitting on the bed, hands in her lap and

smiled when she saw me in the doorway.

"All done in the garage?" she asked.

"I think so. What is making your smile so big?"

"The thought that you would let me take over the big closet and moved your clothes. Have I told you lately how much I love you?"

I moved over to sit beside her and took her hand in mine. "You can't tell me that too many times and I love you too." She turned and put her arms around me in a big hug. If I didn't really realize it before, this made me understand how wonderful it will be to have her here with me every day.

CHAPTER 11

e decided we would still take separate cars to work each day. I never knew when I would be called out and not be coming home when she was. The first morning we took the same ferry but spent the trip from Haven Port to Seattle sitting in her car. That's when she asked me about the notes. Had they stopped?

I really didn't want to get her involved but now that we were living together it seemed like she pretty much had the right to know. I told her about all the notes and she just sat and looked at me while I talked. Then she said, "Can't you do something to find out who is sending these?"

"I so wish I could. We've found no finger prints that were usable. The hair we found was not identifiable, and the guy that delivers notes here to the house hasn't been found. Got any other ideas about where or who to look at?"

Nancy smiled at me and reached over to take my hand. "If I do get an idea I'll call you or just tell you when I see you."

I smiled back at her and squeezed her hand, then went to get back into my car as the ferry was just pulling into the dock in Seattle. A new workday was about to start.

CHAPTER 12

My day was pretty full. Back to Everett and we finally had enough to arrest the guy that took the bank truck. Seems he was pretty drunk when he decided to stop at the bank. He went in, deposited his paycheck then when he came out he just climbed into the truck and drove it away, much to the surprise of the two guards that were in the back of the truck. The problem we were having was finding this driver after he left the truck when the guards finally got him stopped. He'd just got out of the truck and walked away, disappearing into the crowd of people coming out of a theatre. Seems he walked home and told his girl friend he'd been riding in a nice truck. Since he was so drunk she just put him to bed and then she packed up her stuff and left his apartment. This was becoming too much of a repeated action for him. Get paid, get drunk and come home to sleep. When she heard on the news about the truck being driven away from the bank, she called her Uncle who was a policeman in Everett and told him the story. Finally, this case was about to end. Today was the day the Everett Police would pick him up at his job site and I was just here representing the Armored Car company that had their headquarters in Seattle. My partner couldn't be here because he was in court today explaining why he'd arrested a lady that beat up her husband so bad he still couldn't walk, so it was just me winding this up.

After the truck driving guy was safe in the hands of the jailor in Everett, and all the paper work had been signed and I had my copy, I drove back to my office. I'm so glad this case was over and now I could concentrate of something else. It was already four o'clock by the time I parked and entered my office. I gave the paperwork I'd gotten to the officer at the desk in my division, and asked her to inform Jack, my partner, that this case was closed. She would also inform the Armored Car company. They'll be happy too.

When I got back to my desk I found a note from my Boss. It said, "See me when you get in."

The Boss's office is down the hall and it has windows that surround him. It's like he's in a glass bowl. He saw me coming and motioned me in and to a chair across from his desk.

"Just heard the Everett Bank Truck case is finished. Or at least an arrest was made. Good job. Now let's talk about those notes."

We spent the next half hour talking about when the last note was delivered, about the notes in my house and Nancy's house, and the fact that now the local Sheriff was involved. He didn't disapprove of any of this but I knew something was on his mind when he said, "Are you afraid?"

I didn't know how to really answer this. I wasn't afraid, but I was concerned about being threatened and I told him so.

The Boss said, "I know you've done some research but haven't found anyone you would suspect. Am I right?"

I nodded my head yes.

"Is your lady friend Nancy afraid?"

"I don't think so. I haven't really talked to her about this. I don't want her to worry."

The Boss look at me and said, "Well, I think you should talk to her. Are you two living together yet? Planning to get married?"

I smiled at him. "Living together but no marriage plans at the moment."

"She is already involved if she's that close to you. I think you should start talking to her and find out what she thinks. It's only fair she knows all about this, in case she needs to protect herself."

I hadn't thought about it in those terms. What if she got hurt because of these jerks that are doing this BE AFRAID stuff? "What do you think I should do?" I asked him.

We talked for another half hour and he had me convinced that she should be up and running on everything I knew about this. I agreed and I'd talk to her tonight. Now it was a little after five o'clock and I decided I would go home, hoping she would already be there.

CHAPTER 13

George Thistle was on the phone to his client. "Yes sir." Then he listened again. "Yes sir." Then he listened for a couple of minutes and said, "Yes sir. I can do that. When do you want it to happen?" His facial expression changed when he heard the man on the other end of the phone say, "As soon as possible."

After he hung up he realized he was perspiring and sweat was running down his face and dripping onto his suit coat. He took his handkerchief out of his pants pocket and mopped his face. *Wow. The end was getting closer and about to happen.*

CHAPTER 14

When I got home Nancy was there. What a wonderful feeling it is to come in the front door and see her standing in the kitchen. Another treat was that she'd put a beef pot roast in the oven for dinner and I could smell that as I crossed the room to take her into my arms.

I fixed us a martini and we sat at the kitchen table drinking it while we waited for our dinner to cook, and this seemed like a good time to address the notes.

I told her what my boss had said today and then about all the notes and what I'd found out about them, which was very little. She sat there taking it all in and then said, "I might have an idea for you to look into too."

She got up and fixed us another drink. When she sat it down in front of me she said, "Remember the two guys that were arguing at lunch the other day?"

I nodded.

"Well I think I recognized one of them." Then she told me this story: "A little over a year ago, just a month or so before we started going out, I was helping this lawyer from Montana negotiate a settlement with a local food chain. It was an accident in one of their stores where an elderly man fell because he was 'tripped up' by a display in one of their aisles. The guy was from Kalispell and was visiting in Seattle and when he went home his daughter made him contact a lawyer to sue the store because this guy couldn't walk after the fall. This lawyer was Peter Bennett also from Kalispell. He was not licensed in Washington so he asked my old boss, remember Thomas? Well, he asked Thomas to help him get this done. Thomas assigned me to work with Peter and although it took almost sixteen months, it finally ended with a settlement that they approved of. And wonder of wonders, this old guy could walk again. Anyway, the guy that was standing with the fat man looked like Peter and brought back some pretty bad memories."

I stood up and moved to take her into my arms because she looked so distressed, but she said, "Wait. There's more. While we were doing this investigating and work up for the trial, Peter decided this case made us a couple, and he took me out to dinner two times and suggested strongly I come back to his hotel room, etc. I turned him down as graciously as I could but I really didn't like the guy. He was brash and not kind to those people we were interviewing and working with, and in truth, he's what gives lawyers a bad name. I finally had to tell him I was involved with someone. You and I had just started going out, and it made him very mad. He accused me of leading him on and getting his hopes up about us being a couple. I never did that because I never liked him, but when he went back to Montana he left me a note that said, "You and I will end up together. You'll see."

I asked her if she saved the note and she said no. "I wanted no connection with him and since he was gone I just tried to forget he existed. Now I'll take a hug."

I was still standing beside her and as she stood up I put my arms around her, and she put hers around me, and we had a long, loving hug. I really do love this lady and I will see if this note to me stuff is part of her bad memory and take care of it. I didn't tell her that, but I think she knows it. Well, the way she hugged me back, I know she knows it.

Sheriff Ken was in his office when I called the next morning. "Got a few minutes to talk," I asked. He did and we spent some time talking about this guy in the rain coat that was delivering notes. Ken didn't personally know of this guy but he said he'd ask around and let me know as soon as he found out something. I sighed in relief. Someone to help me when I didn't even know where to start.

CHAPTER 15

The next day Sheriff Ken parked in front of Murph's Restaurant and Bar and went in. He was starting his inquires. He'd already talked to his deputies about watching for and looking for this guy wearing a woman's blue rain coat with the red and blue plaid lining, and was hoping Murph or some of his customers might know of this guy.

The three guys from St. Joseph's Retirement Home were sitting at the bar. Steve, George and Larry took a walk down to Murph's every day as part of their constitutional and had coffee, or if they came in the afternoon, sometimes they had something stronger.

Ken sat down at the bar and after he got his coffee set in front of him, he told the guys and Murph about the man in the raincoat. "Ever see this fellow around here?" he asked.

The three men said no and were still shaking their heads when Murph said, "What's this about a fellow in a rain coat? What are you working on, or can you tell us?"

Ken took another drink of coffee and said, "Well I can't tell you names but it's about a break-in and the witness saw this guy. She didn't call 911 because she thought the raincoat guy was maybe part of a repair team. She's an older woman that was suffering from allergies and had taken some medication so..."

George said, "Boy allergies can be blamed for lots of things and so can their medications." He was smiling and remembering that as a teen-ager he took something for his Spring time discomfort that gave him really wild dreams. Dreams about women that he never could imagine before, but remembered the dreams fondly, even now.

Larry looked at him and smiled too. *George is a much deeper person than I thought.*

"Have the deputies seen this guy around?" asked Murph.

"No, not yet, but if he's still here, they will. Especially Ethan. He thinks he's the Barney Fife of Haven Port and he'll be sniffin' around all the bars and public places he can."

The bar started to fill up as the lunch hour approached and Ken decided he'd go look a little too.

Maybe start by checking out the ferry line. The ferry leaving for Seattle happened about every hour and a half, and it was only thirty minutes until the next one left. A check of the on-going traffic wouldn't hurt. He took a last drink of coffee, laid a dollar bill on the bar and left.

Murph was busy taking orders and serving drinks and the three buys from St. Joseph decided they should leave too. They each laid some money on the bar next to their cups and went out the front door in single file. They went to the corner and turned to walk back up the sidewalk they traveled almost every day. Once to come to Murph's Bar, and then to go back to their apartments at St. Joseph's. Today's visit had come with a story about the blue rain coated guy. Something new to talk about.

CHAPTER 16

George Thistle decided another note for Harry was in order then he'd get the final act plan started. He dialed his note delivering guy on his cell phone. No answer. He looked at his watch and saw it was only eight-thirty. Maybe it was too early for him so he'd try again later. He'd have to get the note ready first anyway, then he'd find someone to deliver it. And this started him thinking about where this note should end up. They'd done windshields, in Harry's house twice, well, why not another delivery by a stranger. And this time to his lady friend.

It was after lunch and Nancy was in her office when a secretary came in. "This just got delivered by a messenger for you. The envelope is blank and the guy just came in, laid it on my desk and said, "This is for Nancy Reynolds, and left."

"Did you notice what messenger service it was?"

"Yes, but not one I've heard about before. General Messenger Service was on the back of the guy's jacket."

"Hmmm," said Nancy and she took the envelope by the edges and laid it on her desk. This was something she needed to talk to Harry about and right away.

I answered my cell phone after the third ring. It was laying on my desk and I was a couple of steps away, up by the file cabinet when it rang. I was surprised when he looked to see who was calling and it showed Nancy's number.

"Hi. What's up?" I said when I answered. Then I listened and said, "I'll be right over. I know you know about not touching it, right?" I was already walking out the door, phone to my ear.

While Nancy waited she went out to the main desk and asked for an evidence bag. They had stack of these in the cabinet behind the desk and without a question or inquiry, she received a bag that was see-through plastic, had a zip lock, and was the size that could easily hold a page of paper 8-1/2" by 12". She took it back to her office and opened the bag as she walked. Then she picked up the envelope by the edges again and put it into the bag and zipped it shut. She was still standing by her desk holding the bag when Harry came through her office door.

Nancy handed me the bag and said, "I think this is a message for you."

She was smiling and as I took it from her I said, "I'm so sorry you are involved in this," and I leaned over and kissed her cheek.

She said, "I'm so sorry you are in this too, but we'll get passed this soon," and she moved toward me and gave me a short hug. As she stepped back I once again marveled at my luck of having her in his life. "I'll talk to you soon," I said as I left.

It was then Nancy sat back down at her desk and the tears came. She was so afraid for him.

I took the bag with the envelope directly to my evidence processing department. The sign on the door only said Testing but I knew from experience they could find fingerprints easily too.

In about thirty minutes I had an answer. There were prints on the envelope. Some were unknown and probably female. I figured they were from the secretary that delivered the note to Nancy. The others were identifiable because they belonged to a known felon with a record. I made a note of his name and the address on file, then took the note out of the envelope to see what it said. GIVE THIS TO YOUR BOY FRIEND. IS HE AFRAID YET? Now I was really mad. This was going too far, and to involve Nancy was outside of my limit. I picked up the envelope and note and went to the Boss's office. I was going to need some time to track this down and get it finished. Once and for all I wanted whoever was behind this to know that involving Nancy was not only going too far, but was above and beyond my tolerance level.

CHAPTER 17

When I got back to his desk I had a plan. The next step, was to call Sheriff Ken and fill him in. After I did this I knew my next step, was to track down the delivery guy. His name was Swifty Bergan and the address listed for him was at the homeless shelter down on the water front. That's where I headed.

I finally found a place to park and went in and talked to the Director.

After verifying my identity and looking at my badge he said, "Swifty lives here sometimes but I thought someone told me he died. Let me check." He picked up the phone and in less than a minute was finished and turned to Harry. "I was wrong. He's still living here off and on and at the moment he's here. Want to talk to him?"

Of course I did.

The director came out from behind his desk and motioned me to follow him. As we went down the hall to the stairs he said, "Guess I got some miss-information. Does Swifty have a problem that the police are interested in?"

"Just need some information from him," I said.

"Good. He's a talker so stand by for lots of information," he said as we got to the top of the stairs and went toward a large room that held several men. It was like a living room. Lots of soft chairs and the TV was re-showing a Mariner's baseball game. Some of the guys were watching it and some were just sitting there with their eyes closed. As they entered the Director said, "Anyone know where Swifty is?"

Everyone except a fellow in a corner chair that had his eyes closed, shook their heads no.

"Oh, there he is," and the Director walked over to only one that hadn't responded. I was following.

The Director reached down and touched the shoulder of the maybe-sleeper. "Hey Swifty. You have a visitor."

I was beside the Director and could see this man feign waking up, and I could smell his body odor from three feet away. Then when he spoke, I could smell his really foul breath.

"Oh. Sorry I was asleep. Where's my visitor? Who is it?"

Everyone in the room was listening now. Something different in their day and some were wondering if Swifty was in trouble again.

"I'm your visitor. Is there somewhere private we could talk?" I said.

The Director said, "Sure. Come downstairs and use one of the meeting rooms."

Swifty stood up and I was surprised at how small a man he was. His frame was almost that of a twelve-year-old child and he was only about five foot two inches tall. Along with the stoop in his shoulders, he also looked pretty fragile. The three of us went down the stairs and back towards the front door. The Director stopped in front of a door with a big window across the front of the room. "Use this room as long as you need to," he said and went across the hall to his own office.

I opened the door and motioned Swifty to enter, then I followed. We both took chairs at the table. Swifty sat at the end, facing the interior window, and I sat down facing him with the corner of the table between them.

I spoke first. "I am a detective with the Seattle Police Department. Today you delivered a message to a lawyer on fourth avenue. Do you remember that?"

Swifty took off his baseball hat and wiped his eyes with the back of his hand. "Yeah. I do. Left it at the desk for a Nancy somebody."

"Who gave you the note to deliver?" I was getting excited. Here was some concrete information.

Swifty took another swipe at his eyes with his hand and said, "I was walking down the street and a big fat guy asked me if I wanted to make ten dollars. I said 'doin' what? He said "Just wear this jacket and take this envelope upstairs, leave it at a desk on the second floor and say it's for Nancy Reynolds. I did that, went back to the street and the fat guy took back the jacket and gave me two fives. Don't know the guy but see him around sometimes. Like down by the ferry the other day and then once in the lobby of the Municipal Building."

"Would you know him if you saw him again?" asked Harry.

"Yeah, I think so. Unless he loses about a hundred pounds," said Swifty.

I decided to take a chance and asked, "Do you know a guy that wears a woman's raincoat that is light blue and has a plaid lining?"

Swifty once again took off his hat and this time just wiped his wrist across his forehead. "There is a guy here at the shelter that does that sometimes. He's a skinny guy that also wears rubber rain boots even if it's not raining. Don't know his name and haven't seen him lately but the director might know more." Then Swifty smiled an almost toothless smile and said, "Need to talk to him too?"

"I might," I said. "If you can find him it's worth twenty dollars for you."

"I'll surely keep an eye out. He usually comes in on the week-ends. Don't know where he goes in between. How can I find you?" Swifty was already planning on getting the twenty bucks.

"Here is my card. If I don't answer the phone please leave a message about where I can find you, okay?" I reached into my jacket pocket and pulled out a business card. "The number on the bottom is my office. The other number is an answering service."

Swifty took the card and looked at it, then nodded and put it into his shirt pocket. "Hope I'll be talking to you soon. Do you need me any further?"

"No I don't think so."

Swifty smiled his toothless grin again. "Okay then, I think I'll go get some food and then walk back down here." He stood up, offered his hand to me and we shook. Then Swifty walked out of the room and out of the front door of the building.

I went across the hall to the Director's office, only to find out he'd gone to lunch too. As I walked back to my car I called Nancy. Yes, she could go to lunch and I drove up to get her. We had lots to talk about.

CHAPTER 18

I'm one of those guys that is usually aware of whoever is around me and I noticed that after we arrived at the restaurant and got seated, a very thin man came in and was sitting on the patio where he could see us. Nothing really notable about him except that he kept staring directly at us like he was trying to listen in on our conversation. Nancy's back was to the outside seating, so when I reached over and said in a low voice, "I think you have an admirer on the patio," she turned around just as the guy was walking out of her sight toward the back of the building and the outdoor bar.

"I don't see anyone I know," Nancy said as she turned back around. "What did they look like?"

"It was a guy. Very thin. Dark hair and black glasses. Oh well. I'm happy when others see what a beautiful girl I have with me."

Nancy's shoulders drooped as she leaned in to talk. "That could be him. That lawyer from Montana. Should I go out on the patio and look?"

"Not without me," I said, and as I stood up, so did Nancy.

We moved toward the patio area but Harry was first out the door from the main room. He looked to the right toward the outside bar area and couldn't see the man. Nancy was right behind him and said, "Well, he isn't here now. Where does this patio go? Around the building?"

I didn't know but said, "Let's go back in and we'll ask the waiter."

As soon as we were seated the waiter came over. "Did you want to move outside?" he asked?

I smiled at him. "No. Just thought we saw someone we knew. Where does that patio go? Around the building?"

"No sir. It goes back to the rest room doors and I think there's an equipment storage room back there too." He still had a questioning look on his face.

"Still want to have lunch?" I was looking at Nancy.

"Yes I do," she said. "He's not going to ruin my daily life with his games. But I think I'll sit on the other side of the table," and she was smiling as she got up and moved.

The waiter was smiling now too. He wondered what sort of game these two were playing but as he wrote down their order he noticed a guy from behind them in the other room that was really interested in this couple too.

CHAPTER 19

Over lunch I brought Nancy up to speed on what I'd learned at the shelter from Swifty. "I believe this fellow. He was matter of fact and when he told me that a fat guy gave him the envelope to deliver, I remembered that one of the two guys that were arguing down the hill the other day, that ones where you thought you recognized one of them? Well, the other guy was pretty fat. Do you remember that too?"

"Yes I do, and now I'm sure the other one was Peter. He had a habit, when he was upset, of jabbing that person in the chest with his fingers. Now he's here and I'm afraid not only for you but for me. Am I being paranoid?"

Peter was watching them and saw Harry reach over and take Nancy's hand. He thought, *Hope you enjoy this one last moment. Your time is getting very short,* and he walked out of the door onto the street. His car was parked a short distance away and when he got into it, he just sat there. His heart was racing with the thought that she would soon be alone and be his.

CHAPTER 20

As lunch was ending both Harry and Nancy were not anxious to leave. They were worried about what might be waiting for them on the street and maybe at home even if they weren't voicing it to each other, so they made a plan. They'd stay in Seattle tonight at the safe house Harry knew about. It was a condo on Capital Hill, a neighborhood East of Seattle. He called his Boss and got it arranged. Both of them needed to go back to their offices to finish things that were on their desks and at four-thirty, they would meet in Harry's office by the front door. Nancy would be escorted there by two of her in-house security guards, one of which was an ex-Marine and Harry had lots of confidence in his abilities. It was only two blocks away but two block was a long way sometimes.

When Harry got back to his office he called the Director at the residence he'd been to this morning and asked him about the guy Swifty told him about. "I understand he likes to wear a light blue raincoat and rain boots even when it's not raining."

"Oh, yeah. I know who that is. Doesn't come here regularly, only when his Mother throws him out of the house. Can I call you back? I need to check with the staff and the records to give you more information?"

"Well I'll only be her for about an hour. Will it take longer than that?" Harry asked.

"No I don't think so. Just a few minutes, but I have to leave my office to talk to ..."

"Okay. Got my number?" Harry asked, and got a reply that the Director still had his card so we were all set.

CHAPTER 21

In less that fifteen minutes my phone rang and it was the Director.

He said, "This is what I can tell you about the raincoat guy. He does come here sometimes but not on a regular basis. His name is Timmy Ingram. He isn't retarded but is a little slow on the uptake sometimes, especially in conversations. He's a follower too. He'll hang out with anyone that tells him he should. His home is in Tacoma but when he and his Mother fight, he comes here to sleep. While he is staying here he walks the streets a lot and hangs out down by the ferry, because he says he likes boats. Don't think he has a job. His age is around twenty-five we think, but he might be a little younger or older. When we asked him his date of birth he's give a couple of different answers. He says he likes to wear the rain coat because it was his grandmother's and she gave it to him when she was sick before she died. Don't know why the boots come into play. Does this help?"

I said it certainly did, but if he saw this guy would he please contact me so I could talk to him? He's not in trouble but I need some more information.

The director said he'd make a note of it and then we hung up.

CHAPTER 22

At four-thirty I was down by the front door and watched as Nancy and her two guards walked up to the building and came in. She was carrying a small bag she kept at her office for those times she had to work late or just in case she needed a change of clothes. I was carrying my shaving kit that I kept here for the same reason. No clothes but my face would look clean.

I thanked the guards and Nancy went with me to get into my car in the garage. A couple of other policemen and one other detective were on the elevator with us. Two of the policemen knew about this problem I was having, and walked with us to my car. On the windshield was an envelope. I wasn't really surprised but I am so tired of this stuff.

Jeff, one of the cops asked me if I wanted him to get it off the car and I said yes but be careful of fingerprints. He walked over and picked it up by the edges. This was a bigger envelope than the others. This one was legal size. He handed it to me and I'd already gotten out the plastic bag from my coat pocket and we put it in. I'd look at it later.

Nancy and I got into the car and I backed up while the uniforms watched. I was glad they were there to pay attention to us. As we left the garage I was being very vigilant to watch for anyone following us. We headed up to Capitol Hill and although I knew where the condo was located, I took us on a ride all the way down I-5 to Bellevue then cut back down through some neighborhoods and finally ended up at our overnight place to stay. There was also an under-the-building parking lot and that's where I went, found the assigned space for 303 and parked. The elevator was a couple of spaces down and I put the card I had to activate it into the slot. I for one was breathing a lot easier as we got to the apartment door and was inside. It was only two rooms. The large room held a small kitchen on one wall, and living room, then there was the bedroom with attached bath. Plenty of room for the night. There were no balcony or windows that opened so I liked that feature too.

We put our bags on the bed and I went to look in the kitchen. There was canned soup and crackers on a shelf, and in the fridge was apple juice and orange juice to drink. So, dinner would be tomato soup and crackers and juice. Could be worse. Didn't want to do take-out for obvious reasons.

Nancy came to look in the kitchen too and took out a big bottle of apple juice. She poured two glasses full then put the lid back on for later, and the bottle went back into the fridge.

"Let's have cocktails in the living room," she said and headed that way with both glasses.

One of the wonderful things I have come to love about Nancy is her way of going with the flow. I followed her and we sat down on the couch. Just another day of unwinding after work.

Sometime around mid-night Nancy's phone rang. She'd put it on the bedside stand next her side of the bed and of course it woke her up. It rang two times and she pushed talk in the middle of the third ring. "Hello," she said. There was no one on the other end speaking. Finally, she hung up and she said she could hear breathing but no voice. "That's something stupid that Peter would do," she said to me as she put the phone down. Then she picked it up again and turned the ringer off. "Don't need any more of those calls do we?"

I agreed and as she turned to get under the covers again I took her in my arms. Her protection was uppermost in my mind.

CHAPTER 23

The next morning, I called my Boss. It was about eight-fifteen and usually I'm in the office by now so I wanted to reconfirm that I was out for the day.

When he answered I said, "Good morning. This is Harry. Got the day off and just reminding you."

The boss said, "Glad you called. A guy that says he is the Director for the men's homeless shelter down by the waterfront called. He said the guy you're looking for is there now. He's told the guy he can't leave until you talk to him and wants to know how long that will be."

"How'd he get your number?" I asked.

"Well I think he couldn't get a response from you so he just called headquarters and asked for someone that knew you. Are you planning to go down there?"

"Someone has to and I guess it's me. I'll let you

know what happens." My Boss said okay and we hung up.

Nancy and I were having another glass of juice. There was a coffee maker and coffee but no filters for it. Since I don't really enjoy chewing my coffee grounds, we decide juice would work until we had breakfast. Our discussion was about should she go with me. She was nervous about being alone and I was nervous about leaving her so we both gathered our stuff, and went down to my car. It was still parked in the same place as I expected to see it, and no note on the windshield. All of that was good news. We got into the car and made our way down to the shelter by the water. On the way we decided she would go with me and act like my secretary. I gave her the notebook from my glove compartment, and she pulled a pen out of her purse. When we got there we found plenty of parking because of the early hour. I've found that tourists don't usually start invading our attractions in downtown Seattle until around ten o'clock on weekdays. Weekends are different. Don't plan to find a parking place anywhere on, or very near the water , from Saturday after eight AM until really late on Sunday night. Seattle residents know these rules and we avoid trying to park on week-ends anywhere down-town. Even the week-days are iffy but worse as the weeks almost over.

I parked right in front of the place that housed

these so-called homeless men. We went in and I told the girl at the desk that I had an appointment with the Director but before she could call him he was walking into her area.

"Saw you come in. Hello Harry. How you doin' today?" he said.

"Doin' okay," I said and turned to Nancy. "This is my secretary Nancy. She's riding with me today."

The Director said, "Welcome Nancy," then he looked at me. "Want me to get Timmy and bring him down to the same room you were in last time?"

"Sure, if it's not too much trouble."

"Okay. You go over there and I'll go get him from his room. You might have to turn on the lights too." He smiled as he left.

We were settled at the table when Timmy Ingram and the Director returned. Timmy's hair was sleep arranged, with a flat spot on one side and standing up on the other side. He looked at me then Nancy and said, "I don't know these people."

The Director said, "I know you don't but this gentleman is with the Seattle Police Department and he needs some information from you. You can help him, right?"

"Who is she," he said, referring to Nancy.

I stood up and said, "She is my secretary and will take notes. You are not in trouble but you have some info I need to solve a case. I think you can help me. Will you try?"

Timmy put both arms up in the air and stretched. "Okay and then I'll go back and finish my nap."

The Director left and Timmy sat down across from Nancy. He smiled at her and she smiled back. "Okay, what's your question?"

I said, "Do you remember going to Haven Port on the ferry?"

"Yep."

"Do you remember what you did over there?"

"Which time?" Now Timmy was yawning but not behind his hand.

"Been there more than once?" I asked.

"Sure. I like to ride the ferry and I had some business to do a couple of times."

"What kind of business? Delivering stuff?" I asked.

"Well, not really stuff. Once I had to put an envelope under the door at this guy's house. Another time I had to use a ladder I found by the house and put another envelope on the closet door with a piece of tape."

"Where did the envelopes come from?" This was going slow but I was getting information. Now I was hoping to get down to the nitty-gritty.

"Well, I met this fat guy on the ferry when I riding one time and he said he'd pay me ten dollars each time, to put these envelopes where he told me to, but I had to bring him proof that it had been done." He yawned again and stretched out his arms above his head. "I used my cell phone to take a video of me putting the envelope under the door and a picture of the last one taped to the closet door. That's all the proof he needed and he gave me the twenty bucks when I showed it to him."

"Where did you meet with him to show the proof?"

"I went to his office building and we met in the lobby."

"Do you know his name?" Now I was getting anxious to get to the real information.

"No. Didn't get his name. I was just supposed to wait there in the lobby around four o'clock in the afternoon, and he would come down from his office and find me."

"Did you have to wait long?"

"I got there at ten minutes to four and he got off the elevator about five after. He gave me the money and said he didn't have any more jobs for me at this time. We said good-bye and he went back up the elevator and I went to get the bus home."

"Would you know him if you saw him again?" I was hoping.

"I think maybe, but since he said there were no more jobs, I'll probably never see him again." He looked at me like 'didn't you hear me say that.

I had one last question: "Timmy would you give me your address and phone number in Tacoma?"

"Sure," he said and looked at Nancy as he told us the numbers and street name and zip code.

"Do you want Nancy to read it back to you?"

"No. She looks smart and I think she wrote it down. Didn't you see her do that?"

"Yes I did, and thank you for the information. Do you remember the name of the building you went to for your money?" If I could only get this bit of information, I'd be really cooking.

"Uh huh." There was a pause as he yawned again then looked around the room for a few seconds. Finally, he looked back at me and said, "It's the building on the corner of Second and Seneca. It is mostly a bank building but there are some other offices there too."

Bingo. "Thank you. Now you can go back to your sleeping," I said and without a word he stood up, went out the door and turned toward the stairs. Boy was the Director right. He wasn't really mentally slow, but a little different in his communicating.

Nancy and I went to tell the Director we were finished then we went back to the car. When we were in and were moving I said, "Want to go get breakfast?"

"I'd rather wait until lunch if you don't mind. I'm not expected back to work today so we could even go home if we wanted to.”

I smiled. I was thinking the same thing and headed for the ferry. As we neared the entrance I realized that is exactly where we shouldn't go and I drove past the ferry and while I was moving up the hill back toward my office I told Nancy my plan. She agreed so I pulled over and parked on the street and got my cell phone from my jacket pocket. I dialed and in a few seconds my Boss was saying, “Hello. Where are you?”

Our conversation was short but he let me know that he'd expected I'd need some help after my morning interview.

“Are you being followed?” he asked.

“Don't think so,” I said then checked the rearview mirror, and since Nancy could hear the conversation, she was checking her side mirror too.

“I think you should come back to the office. Can you do that?” the Boss asked.

“Sure. Why?” I asked.

“You know the safe-house you were in last night, well it was broken into about half an hour ago. The security camera caught a picture of the guy and I'd like you to see it.”

“On my way Boss. Can someone meet us as we enter the building just in case I am being followed?”

“Yes. The usual routine,” said the Boss and I started my car. This was becoming a really convoluted case. I reached over and took Nancy's hand.

We stopped at a red light and I said, "Don't worry. We'll be protected very soon." She smiled but didn't say anything.

As we entered the garage on the street level, a police car moved in behind me and blocked the entrance. I went up to the third level and parked as close to our door into the offices as I could. We both got out and quickly walked to the door where a uniformed guard was standing. He opened the door for us and after we were inside he said, "Anyone we need to watch for?"

Nancy took a step toward him and said, "Yes. Tall man, about six foot two, dark rimmed glasses, black hair, and his ears stick out a little more than normal. Name is Peter Bennett and he is a lawyer from Montana. He is not to be trusted. I would search him immediately because he usually carries a small gun in his pants pocket."

I was so impressed with her thoroughness and professionalism. I knew she was scared but she really did step up and put on her professional side to handle the question.

The officer nodded that he got that information and closed the door. I put my hand on Nancy's arm and guided her towards my Boss's office. She was all business now. No more victim. Wish I was feeling that way too.

CHAPTER 24

own in the garage the police car moved away from the entrance and backed into a parking place. He looked at his phone and saw the warning about a tall, thin man that might try to enter this way, and as the he got out of the car he saw a man walking up to the entrance. Since this wasn't normal, he approached the man and said, "Sir. This is not an entry. The entry to the building is around to the right. Not very far but ..."

The man looked at him and kept walking into the garage. "Got to get to my car," he said, and was moving forward at a fast pace. The man had on a stocking cap that covered his hair and no glasses but the Officer decided not to take a chance and moved toward him. *Better safe than sorry*, he thought as he took the man by the arm and guided him toward the door into the building. The man looked around but didn't resist. That was strange too.

The regular garage guard was watching this all happen, ready in case he was needed. He made note on his clipboard about the incident and thought, *Weird stuff happening today.*

Upstairs Nancy and Harry were sitting in the Boss's office.

"I didn't see anyone following us either to or from the Shelter on the waterfront but now that I know our last night's sleeping place was broken into, I'm much more concerned that this guy is getting either more aggressive or anxious or something. Maybe more dangerous." Harry was already holding Nancy's hand and he could feel her tension too when she tightened her grip.

The Boss was leaning forward with his arms on his desk and started to say something but was interrupted when the uniformed officer from the garage knocked on his door. He looked up then said. "Come in."

"Sorry to interrupt but I thought you'd want to know about this." Then he explained how a guy tried to walk into the garage and the fact that he had been detained and was in a holding cell. "The description almost fit the perp we'd been warned about but he had on a hat so I couldn't see his hair and he wasn't wearing glasses. We were told that no warrant had been issued but that he was probably packing, and when he ignored my telling him to go around to the front door, well I just helped him continue into the building. Hope this helps."

"Is he in the holding cell that has a one-way window for observation?" asked Harry.

"Yes sir. Want to go look at him?" And they did. The Boss, Harry and Nancy followed the officer back to the elevator and toward the cells.

"Has he taken off his hat yet?" ask Harry.

"Don't know but I could go in and make that happen," said the officer and the Boss nodded 'yes' to him. When they got to the cell, the officer gestured toward the window then went in and asked the man to please take off his hat.

"Why?" said the man. "And why am I here?" And tears started to run down his face.

The officer said, "Why don't you want to take it off?"

The man said, "Because I'm embarrassed by the scar on my head. I've just been to the doctor." He reached up and took off the stocking cap. A big ugly red scar crossed the top of his bald head. "I had brain surgery and found out today I'll probably never grow hair again up there." And he started to cry again. Big sobs. "I'm only thirty-nine and bald. I wish they'd just let me die." He sat down on the chair next to the table and buried his head in his hands as he leaned on them.

Nancy was relieved and also feeling so bad that

this man had to go through this hassle. And that she was the cause of it.

Harry was also feeling sad for this guy but as he turned to the Boss, he realized this was really a job for the doctor they had on call. "Do you think..." he started to say, and the Boss nodded his head yes. He was thinking the same thing and took out his cell phone to call upstairs and get this action going. This guy shouldn't be on the streets for his own safety and a doctor would be where they should start.

CHAPTER 25

It was almost one o'clock when this was man's problem was over for us. We were both not only weary but hungry. "We could order something to be delivered," I said.

Nancy agreed and we went upstairs to my office. I shared it with three other guys but all of them were out now. *Probably to lunch,* I thought. I went over to my desk and pulled out a folder that had menu's in it from restaurants in the neighborhood that would deliver. We decided on ham sandwiches with potato salad from Herman's. Both of us had eaten there before and liked the food. We also ordered milk for our drink then sat down to wait.

Almost half an hour later the Boss opened the door and came in. "We got hold of his wife and she is coming to pick him up. Poor guy."

I started to apologize for all of this unusual stuff

and the Boss stopped me. "Hey, we look after our own and Nancy is almost our own. We'll continue to help you both until this is wrapped up." He moved over to give me a pat on the back then Nancy stood up and went in for a hug.

"Thank you," she said and there were tears in her eyes. Her usual official appearance was wearing thin.

The Boss hugged Nancy then patted her on the back and said as he left, "Be careful out there and we have another safe house for you for tonight. Check with Sam for the key."

CHAPTER 26

Lunch came, and by the time we were finishing, my office mates were back. They all knew of the situation and told us they were there to help if we needed them. "Want us to post a guard at your door while you sleep?" asked Phillip. Both of us said "no thank you" at the same time, then we smiled at each other.

"I think this will be over soon and we can go home to Haven Port," I said and made a mental note to call the Sheriff and fill him in on what was happening. However for now, I needed to go get the information about this nights lodging.

I was back in a few minutes with the key to another condo just north of here. It was on Queen Anne Hill, and along with that key, was a key for a different vehicle. My car would stay in the parking garage until this was over. The new car was a dark blue Ford Ranger. I smiled. Maybe the perp wouldn't consider a pickup as my choice of transportation.

When we got into the truck to leave, I put on a hat the Boss had given me. It was a black Stetson. Nancy laughed and then I suggested he might arrange herself so she wasn't visible through the side window or windshield. "Don't want to give them site advantage if they do recognize me." She agreed and loosened her seat belt so she could lay down on the seat.

"Hope I don't fall asleep," she said. I hoped so too. I wanted someone to talk to as we traveled. Somehow it made me feel safer to hear her voice.

CHAPTER 27

Without an incident we made it up to Queen Anne Hill. The condo was almost at the top of the hill and parking was in the back. We were the only car in the lot but as we walked up the stairs to the second floor Nancy said, "I could get used to this condo hopping. Could you?"

"I might be able to if we could arrange better food supplies." We were smiling as we entered this apartment.

"This is beautiful," said Nancy. "And look at the view."

She was right. The view was of the west side of Queen Anne and even a gave us a look at Puget Sound. "Wow," I said.

I put down my hat and shaving kit on the kitchen counter and looked in the refrigerator. I could see two steaks and some asparagus on one shelf, and on the counter by the sink was a loaf of French Bread. Beside that was two potatoes just right for baking, and a saucer with a cube of butter. In the wine rack was a bottle of wine. I looked and it was Merlot. Perfect. "Look at all the food," I said.

Nancy was in the bedroom and said, "And look at this beautiful bed. I think I know where we will watch TV tonight."

I walked in there and saw the King sized bed that was one of those with the controls that make it fold up at the head of the bed so you can recline and read or watch TV. Another wow. "Maybe we'll just move over here to live," I said.

Nancy laughed and said, "Don't get carried away. I think I'll be pretty happy to just go home. Won't you be too?"

"Yeah I think home is where I really want to be, but for tonight..."

"I agree. For tonight this is wonderful," and she sat down on the bed to test it. She scooted up so her back was leaning on the slanted head-of-the-mattress and she was smiling very broadly. "In fact, right now it's pretty cool too."

I said, "I have to call Sheriff Ken and fill him in on what is going on then I'll be here to join you. Can you stay awake for fifteen minutes?"

"I'll try she said. Maybe I'll just go take a shower. I can see a robe hanging by the door. In fact, there are two of them. Want to join me?"

I said, "Give me ten minutes to make this phone call, okay?"

She said, "Okay. Ten minutes then I'm headed for the shower, with or without you."

I took out my phone and dialed. Ken answered on the second ring and I gave him the details. I also told him I was hoping to be back at Haven Port either tomorrow or the next day. He said to let him know. He'd been driving by my house just checking, and there hadn't been anything out of the ordinary.

I was happy with this news and when we hung up I could hear the water start to run in the shower. Life was getting better.

After our shower we put on the robes that were hanging by the door. By now it was almost five-thirty and we decided to have dinner. I headed for the kitchen and started looking for a frying pan. I thought Nancy was right behind me but when I started talking to her I realized she wasn't. I went back into the bedroom and found her by the closet that held the washer and dryer. She was putting in some detergent and when she saw me she said, "Decided we needed some clean clothes for tomorrow." I hadn't thought about it but internally I agreed and then we went back to the kitchen.

Nancy did the cooking. She cut up the asparagus and sautéed them in butter with garlic salt while the steaks cooked. Neither one took very long. I set the table with silverware and napkins, but left the plates on the counter, ready for the steaks. I also put the bread and butter on the table too, along with the salt and pepper. No steak sauce but I guess we can rough it tonight. I found two wine glasses and opened the Merlot bottle. I was ready and so was dinner.

Dinner was really good. Eating out is good but home-cooked food is better. At least to me and I think it's the same with Nancy.

After we ate we put our dishes in the dishwasher, turned it on and went into the bedroom. Nancy put the washed clothes into the dryer and we settled onto the bed to watch the news and then a movie. I was slipping in and out of sleep when I felt the bed moving down to be flat and ready for a night's sleep. I reached over and patted Nancy's arm and I was gone off to dreamland. This heavy worrying all day is very tiring for me.

In the morning, after we got up and dressed in our clean clothes, we had a cup of coffee.

"I've been thinking about today. We need to find the fat guy and going to his office seems a good way to do that. However, I think it would be better if I called my partner Jack and he went with me. What do you think?" I was sitting at the table and looking at Nancy.

"Why don't you take me back to your office and

I'll wait there while you and Jack do that?" Nancy was smiling at me.

"Good idea I said," although that's exactly what I had planned. "Can we be ready to leave in about fifteen minutes? I'll call Jack and set it up."

Nancy said yes, went and rinsed out our cups, emptied the coffee pot and rinsed it out and said, "One quick stop to put on lipstick," she said and headed for the bedroom.

I called Jack and arranged for him to meet us in the parking garage and to have someone there to take Nancy upstairs. We were ready to start our attack of this day.

I didn't drive into the garage, but pulled up by the door. Jack and two uniforms came out and as Jack got into the truck, the uniforms escorted Nancy back through the garage and up to my office. So nice to have a team on our side.

As we drove to Second and Seneca street I filled Jack in on what was going on. "And this fat guy works in the bank building. Don't know which office but I know the first six floors belong to the bank and there are only eight floor so..."

"So we start on the seventh floor and knock on doors?"

"Well sort of. I think there is a roster on the main floor and that might give us a clue."

"Sounds like you have a plan. Let's get 'er

done," said Jack and we were almost there. Now to find a parking place.

We had to park about half a block away, but that was pretty close, considering it was a week-day. We walked into the building and there was a list of businesses on the wall by the elevators. Right away I saw a Private Investigator's office on the eighth floor. I pointed it out to Jack and we got on the elevator along with five other people. They all got out on the third floor and we'd overheard them talking about this meeting they were going to. Seems IBM wanted to have more control over the computers in the bank, and this was an important decision that probably would be made today. I was thinking, *Everyone has their problems* and was glad I didn't have this one.

We got off the elevator, and just down the hall to our left was the door marked Municipal Investigators where we were headed. Before we could get there, a very fat guy came out of the door. He looked up and saw us and turned like he was going back into the office. I took a couple of long strides and moved between him and the door. "Just a minute please. I think you can help us."

Thistle looked up at Harry and his face went pale as he recognized him. *Now what should I do*, he thought.

I said, "Hello. Are you free for a few minutes? I need to speak to you."

He looked at me and after he cleared his throat he said, "I guess I could be. Want to come into my office?"

"No. Let's talk here, at the end of the hall," I said, and I took his arm on one side, Jack on the other side and we walked him down to the space by the elevator. The nearest office door was the one he had just come out of and we were still holding onto his arms.

"What do you want?" he asked as he looked from one of us to the other. He looked scared.

"Tell me your name and what you do," I said.

"My name is George Thistle and I'm a PI. Now tell me what you want."

"Do you know Peter Bennett?" I was talking low and only about three inches from his face.

"Don't think so. Why do you think I do?

"Because I saw you talking to him down by the ferry. He's tall and has black hair, glasses and big ears," I said.

"Oh that guy. Yes, but his name isn't Peter. It's John. John Hanson. Comes from Montana and has some business here."

"Do you know what his business is?" I asked.

"Who are you and why are you asking me these questions?" Thistle knew who was talking to him but didn't want them to know he knew.

Harry pulled out his badge and held it up to

Thistle's face. "Seattle Police Department. Please answer my question."

"Isn't this a little odd to interrogating a guy in a hall?"

"Would you prefer to go down to headquarters? I can arrange that," and I pulled my phone out of my pocket.

"No, No." Thistle looked worried. "This is just fine. What do you want to know?"

"Are you working for him?"

"Who?"

"For the Montana guy. Are you working for him?" I was getting tired of this guy's evasions.

Thistle looked at me and said, "I need to sit down. Come back to my office please."

I looked at Jack and he nodded, so the three of us walked back to the office door. We were still holding his arms and when we got to the door, Thistle reached over and turned the knob. We went inside and saw a row of desks along the wall. Some were occupied by people on phones and Thistle said to the receptionist, "I forgot something," then walked toward an office at the end of the row and we followed. His office was just a desk, two filing cabinets and two chairs. One was behind the desk and the other in front of it. He walked behind the desk and sat down. Jack followed him, just in case he had something in the drawers we didn't want him to have.

"This guy from Montana. How do you contact him?" I asked.

"Tell me what this is about so I'll know if I should share information please."

I said, "That's not how this works. The way it works is I ask you the questions and you answer. We can still go down to headquarters to discuss this."

Thistle was shaking his head no. "Okay. I'll tell you what I know about this Montana guy. He is trying to scare a guy that took his girl away from him. He thinks that this guy will drop the girl and then he can move back in and get her back. Is that what you want to know?"

"It's a start. How is he scaring him?" Of course I knew but I needed to hear it from someone involved.

"Now this I can't tell you. I found the guy for him and that's all I really can speak to." Thistle was now fidgeting. He moved a pencil from one place to another. Then pushed the telephone to another space about three inches away. He wasn't looking at me either.

I looked at Jack and said, "I think we need to move back to the office. Mr. Thistle may be more inclined to talk to us in a different environment."

Jack said, "I agree. Should I call a car for transport?"

I started to answer when Thistle interrupted. "Listen. This guy from Montana isn't to be trusted. He has already threatened to get rid of the guy involved and I think he thinks I'm expendable too." Now Thistle was sweating. "If he even finds out you were talking to me, I'm afraid for my life."

Now we were getting somewhere. "Do you have a meeting planned?"

Thistle took out a handkerchief and was wiping his face. "He is supposed to call me today with meeting place information and he's going to pay me for what I've done. Then I think I am out of the loop." He wiped his face again because he was still sweating.

I leaned over the desk toward him. It wasn't very wide and I was only about a foot away when I said, "I think we'll go with you to the meeting."

His face went pale and he started sweating even more, if that was possible. It was dripping from his eyebrows and chin. His handkerchief was pretty damp and he pulled out another one from his pocket. It was pretty clear he didn't think this was a good move.

I looked at Jack as a phone started to make the whirring sound they make to get attention without ringing. "Is that your phone?" I was looking at Thistle and he nodded his head yes. "Answer it and put the sound so we can hear the conversation too. Okay?" Again he nodded yes and took the phone from his shirt pocket.

"Thistle here," he said. The speaker had been turned on and we were listening too.

"Do you know who this is?" said the voice from the speaker.

"Yes," said Thistle and he pointed to the phone with his free hand. I nodded yes to let him know I knew it was the Montana guy.

"Meet me down by the Seattle ferry dock in the parking lot. I'll be there in thirty minutes. Can you make that?"

"Yes I can," he said. "It's a big lot. Where?"

"Close to the passenger door on the ground floor. The one on Alaska Way. Know that place?"

"I do," said Thistle. "I'll be there in thirty minutes or maybe earlier."

"Good," said the voice and the phone went dead.

Thistle looked both relieved and concerned at the same time.

"I was wondering, are you expecting more instructions when you meet him?"

Now Thistle was coming completely undone. Tears were running down his fat cheeks and he said, "I'm supposed to bring him a gun that is untraceable."

"Do you have such a gun?" I asked.

"It's in my car but yes. The serial numbers are filed off and the barrel of this gun has been exchanged with a new gun that has never been sold. The barrel was made by a collector I know and only fired in testing. No records of it exist."

"Let's go down to your car. I need to see this gun," I said and as I stood up so did Thistle.

"Do you need to sign out when we leave?"

"No. I'm the boss and I come and go as I please, but we have to hurry to make the meeting in thirty minutes." Thistle moved toward the door with Jack on one side and me on the other.

When we got into the hall, Jack said, "Do you want to call in or want me to?"

"Would you and make some arrangements? I'll go with Thistle and we'll meet you at the Ferry dock."

Jack nodded and as we got to the elevator he was already talking to the office. He

motioned for me to go ahead and he headed for the stairs. I smiled. Another thing to be grateful for, this good partner.

CHAPTER 28

J ack told the Boss what was happening and what we needed. He sent a car with two plain-clothes detectives to pick him up and they would go to the ferry dock. Hopefully to be there before we were.

Thistle and I got down to his car and he said he'd drive. I thought that would be okay but what if he decided to take a side trip. "How about I drive to the meeting since you're so upset?"

He reluctantly agreed and literally crawled into the front seat of his car. Parked next to this was a van that had a whole bunch of electronics in the passenger seat. "Is this van yours too?" I asked.

He nodded yes then said, "It has a small set of office equipment in the front seat. Printer and stuff. I use it when I need to verify stuff I have on my phone, like pictures and things."

Harry decide that this is where his notes

probably came from and made a note of the license plate number. It would probably be evidence too if it came to a court case.

They drove down to the ferry dock and Harry flashed his badge to get through the gate and into the parking lot. When they got out of the car Harry said, "Do you think you can handle meeting this guy on your own? He might be spooked if I was with you."

Thistle thought, *Oh, is you only really knew.* "Okay. Where will you be?"

"Just around the corner. I'll hear and see everything."

Thistle looked and him and thought, *I hope so.*

It had been almost twenty-five minutes when the un-marked car carrying Jack and two suits came around the corner into the parking lot too. Harry motioned to them and started for the other side of the building while Thistle started for the building entrance. He'd go out that way to make the meeting. The suits followed him and Jack followed Harry.

As they walked, Jack said, "Got a plan?"

Harry said, "Yeah. Get this perp into custody and if he dies during a gun fight, oh well."

CHAPTER 29

I looked around the building and saw Thistle standing there as a tall, thin man walked out of the double doors to join him. Harry pulled his gun and came around the building with Jack by his side. The thin man looked up and then said something to Thistle as he grabbed him and pulled him in front of his body.

There was a gun in the thin man's right hand and his left was holding Thistle in a head-lock. "Stay back or I'll let him have it," he said.

"Why? What's he done to deserves that?" I said, and I could see the two suits coming around the other side of the building. Each of them holding a gun too.

"As I slowly approached a Security Guard come out of the building and that distracted the thin man enough so the two suits could rush in and take control. Thistle moved away as they put Peter Bennett down on the ground and hand-cuffed him. Next, they picked him up and marched him around to the squad car that was parked in the lot. It was a well-oiled procedure that almost seemed staged.

We put their guns away and I took Thistle's arm, as we too walked toward the parking lot. Thistle would go back to headquarters too but in a different car.

Jack talked to the police car drivers and both of them moved away. "Want to take a cab back to your truck or what?"

"Yeah. Let's do that and go back to the office. I can't wait to see the thin guy put into a cell and maybe Thistle too for his part in this." I was really feeling relieved as we went to get into one of the cabs that are always waiting for fares from the ferry riders.

CHAPTER 30

We got back to our office in time to see the thin guy going into the interrogation room. Thistle was in another one. My Boss said, "Want to be in on this?"

I said, "Yes, but I need to see Nancy first. Can you give me a few minutes before you start?"

He said yes and I headed for my office. As I walked in she stood up and I took her into my arms. "It's all over honey," I said.

"It is?" He voice was a little shaky. "Tell me what happened."

"I'll tell you the details later but this is a short version. We found the fat guy and he was going to have a meeting with Peter so we tagged along. When Peter pulled a gun the guys subdued him and brought him in. He's in the interrogation room now, waiting for us to talk to him. Want to see him?"

Nancy shook her head no. "If I never have to see him again I'll be happy."

"Then get happy I said. Your wish is my command." Then I thought for a second, "Maybe you'll be needed at the trial but other than that..."

"I'll face that if it happens," she said and then stepped back. "Go do your interrogation job then come back and get me so we can go home. I'll be here waiting."

I leaned over to give her a quick kiss on the cheek. "I love you," I said and went out to do some question asking.

EPILOGUE

Nancy and I have been happily living in Haven Port for the last three months. Two of those as happily married folks. When we got home I called Sheriff Ken and told him how it all turned out. He was happy it was over for us and told me he was happy too. His wife had been away but was coming home next week. I was happy for him too. When you love someone it's really hard not to have them with you so Nancy and I decided to make it permanent too.

It was a lovely wedding in St. Joseph's Chapel and it was a full house. Murph and Lisa, Sheriff Ken and his wife, and his deputies were all there. My brother and his family came and so did Nancy's Mother and her sister and family. Several of the St. Joseph's residents attended too because 'weddings are so special'. We also had the reception there in the upstairs room. It was a wonderful day. We decided to take a honeymoon trip later because Nancy has a big trial coming up and I really need to get back to work.

I finally opened the last note in the big envelope a week after we got home. It was hand written and said, "YOU'LL GET YOUR REWARD IF YOU TRY TO KEEP HER."

I don't think it was intended to be good, but he was so right. I did get a big reward and I'm keeping her.

And... I got some really good news the week after Nancy and I tied the knot. Peter Bennett committed suicide in his cell. Tied several shirts and pants and a blanket together, and hung himself. When I told Nancy she cried. She said it was from relief and I thought it probably was. As for me, I thought it couldn't happen to a better guy.

www.ingramcontent.com/pod-product-compliance
Lightning Source LLC
Chambersburg PA
CBHW070523100726

47907CB00004B/954